We ha
during th
bracelet a
feel myself blushing as they share a chuckle that seems potent with meaning. Mister Caldwell strokes my thigh under the table the entire night and I hear nothing of what is said.

Walking toward the limousine, the older client accompany's us and I feel a flash of uneasiness as my bosses hand tightens on my arm. The parking lot is only dimly lit. Sam the chauffeur get's out of the front seat to open the back door but Mister Caldwell stops him.

"I would like to see the notes from tonight's meeting," the older man says, his eyes steady, direct, challenging.

I blush. "I didn't take any," I stammer.

"Your secretary is a bad girl," he says to Mister Caldwell. I feel my boss turning me, his arm tight around my waist as he bends me over. I see the chauffeur's face watching with interest as I feel my dress sliding up.

WILD TATTOO

LYN DAVENPORT

BLUE MOON

BLUE MOON BOOKS
NEW YORK

Wild Tattoo

Published by
Blue Moon Books
An Imprint of Avalon Publishing Group Incorporated
161 William Street, 16th Floor
New York, NY 10038

ISBN 1-56201-259-2

9 8 7 6 5 4 3 2 1

Printed in the United States of America

Distributed by Publishers Group West

The soft snick of the lock releasing alerts me that he is entering the room. The ultra thick carpeting hides all sound of footsteps, as it does throughout the entire apartment. Time seems to slow to a crawl. Not a sound is heard. My skin becomes sensitized, waiting, hoping for, aching for the touch of his fingers. I lick my lips but utter no sound.

Two voices talk quietly above me, the soft caress of a finger stroking my bare skin at the same time. It begins on my ankle and makes its negligent way up to my breast. My lips part as I begin to breathe quickly. The finger touches my nipple with the weight of a feather. It strokes, strums and caresses till I bite my bottom lip in exquisite torture. Still I am silent. I hear his low, husky laugh.

"You see how she responds?"

"Very nice," a voice answers. Does it have an oriental accent? I can't be certain because I am blindfolded, as I always am when he has important guests. Even though I am bound to the bed I know it is his touch I feel. No one but him ever touches me in my bedroom. There are other rooms for that when it's necessary.

I arrive in New York right after my eighteenth birthday, happy to finally be away from my bitter old aunt who has raised me these past two years since my parents' death. My uncle is a tall, extremely thin man who suffers from senility and lately his addled brain has made him fancy himself a ladies' man. It hadn't helped my aunt's and my strained relationship when my uncle had taken it into his befuddled head that he was entitled to me as payment for raising me. She found me wrestling with him on the living room floor and, of course, claimed it was my fault. A church going man like my uncle wouldn't have ever done such a thing, crazy with senility or not. I was hauled to church and forced to confess to the priest. He decided my aunt was probably right.

Why is an orphan either pitied or mistrusted? Why is it that people don't think of orphans as regular people? How many times have I seen eyes raised to heaven for patience because, you know, she's an orphan. I think that's when I started feeling guilty that I hadn't died with my parents. Maybe it was my fault that I had the flu and missed being in the car with them. Maybe I deserved whatever punishment I received.

I left a week later after he cornered me behind the garage. It's amazing how strong an old geezer can be. Luckily I escaped but that was it. I had no ties holding me and packing up my things, I bid a happy good bye to auntie and crazy uncle and left for the big city. Every small town girl's dream.

I found a decent room at a decently priced hotel and went to the first employment office I found in the telephone directory. The man I spoke with was very businesslike, almost abrupt until reading my application he suddenly became more human.

"Your name is Julia Mae Davis?"

"Yes sir."

He smiles a friendly smile and I relax a little. "Are you from the South Miss Davis?"

"No sir. My mother was though," I add quickly as if it might be important. I feel myself flush with embarrassment. He peruses the paper he holds that tells almost my life's history and pursing his lips thoughtfully, finally lays the paper on his desk. "Miss Davis I have good news for you," he states. "If your skills are indeed as good as you claim," I am shaking my head enthusiastically, "I believe I have the perfect job for you."

"You mean now? Today? I never dreamed it'd be so easy," I say with relief, fleeting thoughts of my not too large amount of savings drifting through my mind.

"Here's the address. I'll call them and tell them you're on your way." He stands and shakes my hand before handing me a slip of paper with the name and address of the company. "Give this to Mister Caldwell when he interviews you."

I am almost hugging myself with suppressed happiness. Can I really land a job my first day in the city? I check the address and am surprised to see a hand written note on it. 'This one is perfect for you.' How sweet of the man to give me a recommendation.

The building is uptown and enormous. I smooth my clothes and quickly apply a small dab of lipstick while looking at my reflection in the glass windows. Taking a deep breath I enter the enormous foyer, trying desperately to appear confident and older. I approach the security guard at the desk. He takes one uninterested look at the paper and instructs me to go to the top floor.

I clutch my pocketbook on the ride up, thankful I am alone in the elevator. I need the time to compose myself. Everything is happening much faster than I thought it would. Where were all the stories of pounding the streets for weeks before landing a job?

The doors open, my heart gives a nervous thump, and I take another deep breath and unknowingly walk out of my old world and into an unknown one. Everything is extremely modern, all muted earth tones and chrome. It is cold, physically and aesthetically. I shiver before I can stop myself. Goose walking over your grave, my mother would have said with a smile. A women in her late fifties sits at a huge reception desk, the phone to her ear, her other hand beckoning me forward. I approach and wait politely, trying hard not to fidget, and a moment later she covers the receiver with her other hand.

"Are you the new girl to replace Susan?"

"I guess so ma'am. The agency sent me over."

"Go in and Mister Caldwell will interview you right now." She waves her hand negligently towards two doors down the hallway and starts conversing loudly before I can inquire which door. I swallow and walk down the hall standing between both. Again I seek her help but she is deep in conversation and I can't catch her eye. Nothing is written on either door.

What to do? Suppose one was a men's room or a private office? How could they have nothing on them? I glance once more at the receptionist but she is still engrossed in her conversation. I catch sight of a man standing behind me, leaning against the wall. I turn to ask his help but instead find myself tongue tied, his eyes appraising me from the top of my head to my feet. I have never felt so naked in my life. My skin turns cold and then hot as I feel the flush creep up my face. Do something, I scream silently to myself but I find myself unable to move and I stand there allowing his eyes to disect me. I watch him push off of the wall he is leaning on and step nearer to me.

"Can't make up your mind which door?" he asks quietly, my eyes still glued to his. I shake my head, feeling foolish but unable to do anything to correct it.

He walks very slowly till he's directly in front of me. I can sense a feeling of control and it makes me uneasy.

"Do you want to be shown the right way?" His voice is not quite a whisper but it seems to brush over my skin silkenly as if it is a physical thing. My breath is shallow, my lips open. "Do you wish me to lead you?"

I can't break eye contact and stare at him as if mesmerized. The touch of his fingers on my arm finally bring me back to the present. I feel my face flame with embarrassment. The last thing I wish to appear is incompetent. This man might even know my potential employer.

"Thank you." My voice is harsh and stammering, just the opposite of what I wish it to be. His sudden half mocking grin makes me blush all over but I allow him to lead me to the door on the left. He drops my arm and I realize it is slightly numb from the pressure his fingers have exerted. He is opening the door and a woman in her mid thirties who is seated behind another desk looks up with an inquiring smile, the smile deepening when she spies the man.

"Good morning Mister Caldwell. I left your mail on your desk and there are no messages." She rises and opens another door that is about ten feet behind her desk. I wish the floor would open up and swallow me whole. This is Mister Caldwell.

"This is Miss. . . . ?

I see the girl looking at me, waiting. I glance at the man and see the amused smile, the eyebrows cocked as he waits for me to answer. I seem to be in some kind of void. Nothing is real. "Davis," I finally manage to get out between stiff lips.

"Miss Davis, Mrs. Porto," he introduces and standing in the other doorway beckons me in. I move like an automaton. Where did all my confidence flee to? You'll lose the job if you don't straighten yourself out. The very thought terrifies me and I make an effort to avoid the disturbing eyes and gather control over myself.

"Sit down Miss Davis. Do you have something from the agency for me?"

I dig in my handbag and offer him the paper across the desk he is sitting behind. He glances briefly at it and I think I see a satisfied smile flit over his lips but it is gone before I can be sure.

"Your skills are impressive Miss Davis."

"Thank you sir. I practiced hard."

"You wished to make sure you had a skill so you could come to the big city Miss Davis?" His voice is low, casual but I find my mouth going dry. I nod and avoid direct contact with his eyes. His very disturbing eyes. They are too intense, too dark, too steady for me to withstand them. "There are many skills a woman can have and survive in this city Miss Davis." Why do I feel uneasy? His voice continues in the same way. "Why did you decide to become a secretary?"

"It's all my school taught," I answer before thinking. I sound like a hick from nowhere.

He steeples his fingers and tilts the chair back. "I see. If there was another way to earn a living and live well would you be interested in it, Miss Davis?"

I finally meet his eyes and they make me feel small, helpless. "I don't know. I suppose it depends on what it is," I say defensively.

"Just so," he answers ambiguously. "Now for your duties. Mrs. Porto is my secretary and handles all the office but I find with a new deal I am working on I require someone who can take dictation accurately, type well and has the dedication to put in the time that will be necessary to bring this deal home. It is important to me and the firm and I need someone who isn't tied up with family and dates. The hours will be quite late sometimes, depending on how the deal is going down."

He pauses for a moment and studies me thoroughly. I feel as if he is undressing me even though his eyes never leave my face. I wonder if he can guess my thoughts and blush. He ignores it but I think I see a strange glint in his eye.

"Are you willing to try this Miss Davis? Will you make yourself available to me whenever I wish?" I can't seem to catch my breath. Is there a double meaning? Is he propositioning me? "The pay is good and of course there's the usual benefits. It will entail going out to dinner with the client quite frequently as well as lunch so you'll save on your food bills. Are you settled somewhere?"

"Not really sir. I'm staying at a hotel for the moment. I haven't had any time to try to find an apartment. I just arrived in town yesterday."

"If you take this job you won't have any time for quite awhile. No friends you could ask to search for you while you work?" I shake my head.

"I don't know anyone in town."

Again I think I see a satisfied smile flit over his lips but it's hard to be sure. "I'm sure we'll be able to work out something so you'll be able to get settled into a place you deserve. Things sometimes just seem to fall into place."

I look to see if he has an underhanded meaning but all I see is him perusing some papers on his desk. I am well aware of harassment. I've watched many talk shows on television and followed the Thomas-Hill hearings closely. My readiness to do battle falters at his complete disregard of me and I feel young and foolish.

"Excuse me," he says with a frown and pushes a button on his desk. "Mrs. Porto please come in here."

I sit and try not to eavesdrop on the business he discusses with his secretary. I look around and see over stuffed black leather furniture. There is a low table in front of two chairs in one corner of the room and a very long couch. A painting is above the couch and I strain my eyes trying to make it out. I feel the blush mounting again. It's a nude man and women in an erotic pose. The man is holding her hands on the floor as he makes love to her. I tear my eyes from it. Why is my heart fluttering?

Nothing else other than his desk. A door leads to somewhere on one wall, another to somewhere else on the other and in front of his desk is the door that leads to his secretary. Behind him are windows. Floor to ceiling that let in enormous amounts of light. I notice the light behind him slightly shadows his face so it is hard to be completely certain of his expression. Mine on the other hand would be well lit and easy to read. I must remember that, I tell myself nervously.

Mrs. Porto gathers up some papers on his desk and smiling at me brightly, briskly leaves the room. He leans back in the chair and places his hands behind his head. "Are you interested in working for me Miss Davis?"

Is there a smirk on his lips? "Yes sir."

He rubs his hands together slowly and again I feel that quick flash of unease. Leave, my mind tells me but I find myself rising and following him to the door on the right. My office, he explains.

It's a small room, barely six feet by eight feet. He murmurs something about needing me close by and how it used to be a closet. The air-conditioning stops it from being stifling but I feel slightly claustrophobic. There are no windows and the overhead light switch is outside the door. The room is taken up completely by a desk and one filing cabinet. There are three hooks in the ceiling, two have hanging plants on them. He sees me looking at them.

"A service changes them every week before they die. I think it makes it more cozy." His eyes are still looking up. "I haven't found exactly what I want to hang from the other hook yet," he says quietly, almost to himself but I feel the gooseflesh rise along my body. He isn't even looking at me. What is the matter with me?

The next two weeks are hectic. I try hard to grasp the details of this megadeal he is trying to work out. Sometimes I sit at my desk for long moments trying to work things out for myself. I do not want to appear stupid. It's uncanny how he always seems to know when I'm puzzled. He'll appear at the door a few minutes later and immediately he's behind me and explaining. There is hardly any room between my chair and the wall but he squeezes in so he can lean over me and show me the charts and figures. It imprisons me firmly against the desk. The first week he did this I braced myself for some sort of come on, some touch that was out of line, but the only touching was an occasional meeting of fingers as we poured over the papers and my head rubbing against his belly if I lifted it too high. I began to trust him but could never quite shake feeling small and insignificant when he towered over me that way. I seemed to be trapped, which was absurd, and helpless, which was even more absurd, yet at the same time I felt surrounded and safe.

The occasional brush of his coat sleeve against my bare arm sent shivers running through me. It titillated me. It made me uneasy. But I still found myself looking forward to it.

We go out to lunch about three times a week and dinner about four times a week. My wardrobe is sorely strained by the beautiful places we dine at. I see Mister Caldwell glance with dismay more than once at my attire but my budget is stretched to the limit. I had planned ahead while still living with my aunt and uncle and my wardrobe is composed of mostly business suits and sensible shoes. The heels are low and comfortable, but fancy enough to be acceptable anywhere.

As he had promised, working late nights didn't leave any time to find an apartment. His different clients are always polite and other than taking notes, I usually stay out of their conversations. Mister Caldwell asks me for figures or names occasionally but I really do little else. I catch one of two eyes lingering on me once or twice but that is all. No one ever makes an improper advance. None seek me out afterwards. A few times I find myself almost resenting it that no one seems interested at all.

I'm not bad looking. True I am young but eighteen isn't jail bait any longer. I have blond hair and light blue eyes. My features are even and while I'm no outstanding beauty I certainly have been referred to as pretty more than a few times. My body is good. My breasts well rounded and firm. My stomach is flat and my waistline is in proportion to the rest of my body. I'm average height and more than one person has told me I have nice legs.

Mister Caldwell always insists on his limousine dropping me off after a late night. Sometimes he'll be with me, sometimes not. He never tries to kiss me good night but has a funny habit of running his finger briefly over my cheek before I leave the car. I find I miss the gesture when he isn't there. I am getting used to the good life.

The third week he walks into my office and shutting the door leans against the opposite wall. I stare at him in bewilderment. His gaze is intense and I become very uncomfortable. My eyes flick towards the doorknob and an amused smile lifts his lips. "Are you afraid I've come to do you harm Miss Davis?" His low tone is almost mocking and I feel the flush crawl up my face. I lower my eyes and stare unseeingly at the papers before me. I have to swallow to work some saliva into my mouth.

"Is there a problem Mister Caldwell?" Why is my voice shaking? Why can he make me so unsettled so easily? He is a handsome man. About six foot with brown curly hair that seems to beg to be touched. My fingers itch to feel it between them each time I see it. His eyes are dark and probing. I always feel he can read my mind and he sometimes surprises me by doing just that. It is upsetting to think you can have no secrets from someone. Especially someone like him. His lips are, seductive is the only word I can think of that describes them. They seem to beckon, to invite. Sometimes they twitch slightly, as if he is getting ready to kiss something. I find myself thinking of kissing those lips, of sucking the slightly fuller lower lip into my mouth and lightly biting it. I clench my legs together and force myself to listen to his words.

"You wouldn't mind doing that for me would you Miss Davis?"

He's been talking and I haven't been listening. I find myself nodding in agreement, to what I have no idea, but anything is better than admitting I've been daydreaming about him and his lips. "Stand up."

I stumble to my feet and awkwardly approach him in the confined space when he crooks a finger at me. He has a tape measure in his hand. "My tailor assures me he can have the clothes ready by first thing next week as long as we get the measurements to him today. The woman he uses is exceptional. Arms up."

I do as he says, trying to unscramble his words. He is ordering me clothes. I must have agreed to let him buy me a few things to wear to the meetings with his clients. I am standing in front of him with my arms above my head and he reaches around me and places the tape measure against my back. His hands come forward and his fingers brush against my breasts. My nipples harden to small pebbles and my breath is fast and shallow. I look over his shoulder, in a panic lest he realizes how even this impersonal touch affects me.

"Big breath," he whispers and I inhale. Am I trying to take a deeper breath than normal to make my breasts seem larger? I feel as if this is an outer body experience. My skin is both numb and exquisitely sensitive to the least touch. How can that be? I feel his hands around my waist, measuring, and start to lower my arms but he is bending forward and if I lower them I will end up with them around his neck. I quickly lift them and keep them there. He is kneeling, measuring from hip to knee and then he looks up and gives me a quick heart stopping smile. It throws me and again I feel like I'm not really here.

"Open your legs."

I do and gulp in air at the touch of his hand on my inner thigh. He stops at the top of my thigh and again measures to the knee. The tops of his fingers brush the crotch of my panties. I am so weak I could fall but then he straightens and turning jots down the numbers. I realize I still have my hands up and lower them. He looks at me and nods. "You should have them by early next week. I appreciate you realizing how important it is to make a good impression. I was afraid you might misinterpret my meaning." He opens the door and turns. I am still standing where he left me. "You can leave early today Miss Davis. We're almost caught up with everything. Have a nice weekend."

I barely make it on shaky legs to my chair. I try to catch my breath and calm down. Every nerve ending in my body is alive, crackling as if electrified. Never have I had such an experience. I clench my legs together, too aware of the hard bud that is pulsating with a need it's never known. My breasts ache and I feel beads of sweat form on my brow.

I start to panic. I have to leave. He told me to leave. If I don't he might come back to see why I'm still here. Suppose he could read my mind right now? I hastily gather up my handbag and shove the papers on the desk into the top drawer. I take a deep breath and try to compose myself.

Opening the door I see him at work at his desk. His head of curly, silky hair, bent over as he reads a paper. He doesn't look up and I hurry to the door. I get it open a mere inch before his low voice reaches me. "What size shoes do you wear Miss Julia?"

"Six and a half," I murmur and then hurry out. Do I hear a quiet chuckle? I nod at Mrs. Porto and rush to the elevator. Please let it be empty. It's not. I keep a smile on my face all the way down and hurry outside the building, barely acknowledging the guard in my haste. I must get home. The need to be inside my room is growing as the minutes tick by. I am getting frantic. I feel I'll start screaming if I don't find a cab and then thankfully one stops and I clamber into the back. I tell him my address in a breathless voice, as if I'd run a long distance. We seem to hit every light, every jam up the city has. I throw some money at the driver, ignore his shout of abuse at the measly tip and rush up to my room. I don't hesitate but strip my clothes off as I head for the bed. I lay down and close my eyes, reliving the sensations in my office. My hand caresses my breasts, tweaking the nipples. It slowly works its way lower on its own and then my fingers make contact with that tiny part of my body that is driving it insane.

Virgin fingers play with a virgin clitoris. I feel my breath coming harder. I am almost panting, ready to scream aloud as my fingers instinctively begin to work harder and faster. Everything centers low in my belly and then creeps lower and lower till I do scream as the feeling builds and builds and then finally, unbelievably, bursts. I lay on the bed, legs spread and limp, hand still soothing myself and I'm in awe. Never had I imagined the powerful feelings that resided inside me. Never had I ever believed they were truly as wonderful as I had read. Books didn't begin to describe it.

Had he called me Miss Julia?

I didn't search for an apartment that weekend. I spent the time discovering my body. I lay on the bed for hours reliving what had happened in my office. Trying to build myself to a pitch so I could reach that wonderful pinnacle of feeling again. I want to know what it would have felt like if he had touched my breasts, had held them. Would it feel the same as my own hands stroking them? Why had no one else ever affected me like this?

I had dated, nothing steady or deep but I had gone down old Mister Bailey's lane a few times with one or two boys. We'd kissed and it had been nice but nothing like what I was feeling now. And he hadn't kissed me. Hadn't done anything but speak to me.

My phone rings Sunday afternoon. I recognize the low voice right away. "I trust I'm not interrupting your weekend Miss Julia but there are some things at the office that have to be taken care of today. I'll see you there at three o'clock." It is after I hang up that I realize he hasn't asked but told me to be there and I'd quietly accepted the order.

I arrive at the office on time and find it empty. There are boxes on Mister Caldwell's desk and as I pass I notice my name on them. At least I assume they are meant for me. They say Miss Julia. Why Miss Julia? I hesitate but find I don't have the courage to open them. After all they are on his desk.

I hastily make my way to my own small office and taking the papers from the top drawer put them in order and start working on the format he probably wants by the end of the day. A short while later my door opens. It suddenly occurs to me he never knocks.

"Didn't you see the boxes Miss Julia?" he asks, brows raised in question. My heart starts a steady tattoo in my chest.

"Yes sir, but. . . ."

"But you needed permission before you could open them." His voice is casual but I sense something else in it. I can't quite define it but it almost seems like a challenge. An intimate challenge. "Do you need permission to do a lot of things Miss Julia?"

His eyes hold mine and I can't break away from the intense gaze. He raises his hand to me and I rise and take it, letting him lead me to his desk as if I have no will of my own. At that moment I don't believe I do. "You have my permission to open the boxes Miss Julia," he whispers from behind me, his breath tickling my ear.

Unsteady hands lift the lid from the top box. I stare as if frozen at the lace and satin garter belts and panties. Matching bras and camisoles lay by their side. I struggle to breath. He reaches over my shoulder and pushes the box to the side, the soft cloth of his sleeve caressing my cheek making my mouth go dry. My nipples harden and begin to ache.

"This is the one we want." He steps to my side and lifts a flimsy piece of cloth from the box, putting it into my hands. "Go in the other room and try this on for size. Here," he says, lifting garter belt, nylons, and panties from the box.

I take them because I can't think of a reason not to. I have agreed to this. I turn toward my office but his fingers take my arm and lead me to the door on the opposite side. I have never seen what's behind it. He opens it and gives me a push in the small of my back and I enter a world of black and white. The ceiling is white, the walls black. I blink. It is disorienting. The carpeting is black. Every piece of lint must show, I think. I try to adjust to the low light. There is a large backless leather couch with high cushioned arms on one side of the room. Spotlights on the ceiling, the only light in the room, shine on two prints on the wall. I stare and then move closer. The prints are large, maybe four feet by four feet. The background is white, the picture done in black ink. One shows a women tied and being spanked, the other a woman being forced to perform fellatio. Because of the angle of the lights, the other side of the room is in deep shadow. I can't see what is there. Run, my mind screams but I hear his voice on the other side of the door.

"We haven't all day. Get a move on."

How does he know I haven't begun to dress? I look at the pieces of cloth in my hand. I'm intrigued by the very skimpiness of the articles. I walk to the couch and drop them on it, the black clothes almost disappearing from view as they settle on the black leather. My fingers work with a will of their own. I no longer feel as if I have control of myself or the situation. I shouldn't do this, I tell myself but my fingers keep on disrobing me. I step out of my clothes as if in a dream. I glance down and my white body almost seems to glow in the light. It is just one more white thing against the black background of the room. I don't really exist. I am as light as air, a person who is flowing. That's it. This is just a dream. A sensuous dream.

The stockings glide up my legs, silky, sheer. I step

into the panties and find they are nothing more than a small diamond shaped patch of cloth with a thong that slides between my cheeks. I look behind me and in the dim light my white rear is bare. Naughtily naked. I feel deliciously daring. I hook the satin garter belt and attach the stockings as if I'd done it all my life. Things go so smoothly in one's dreams. I pick up the dress and raise my arms, visions of that day in my office instantly back in my mind. My nipples ache. The dress slides down my arms. It caresses me as it goes. I give it a small tug and it drifts to my waist. My breasts are supported by a thin piece of rounded wire under each mound. The cloth barely covers my nipples. I look down in wonder. It is so soft. I wiggle my rear and it slides down but not far. The dress ends just above mid thigh. I flush with pleasure. Does one flush in dreams?

I hear a noise and turn, my dream shattering as I see him standing there holding high heels. It isn't a dream. All my self possession flees. I am suddenly embarrassed and awkward. His eyes travel the length of my body. I shiver for no reason. I feel more naked than I actually had been a few minutes before.

"It's not what I wanted but put on the shoes anyway," he whispers, approaching me and holding out black pumps. I take them, anything to have something to do with my hands. His fingers bite into the soft part of my arm as he supports me. How could fingers that had perfectly donned sheer silk stockings a few minutes earlier not be able to hold shoes the right way so they could be worn? I finally get them on and stand before him. I can't raise my eyes to meet his. I want this to end. I want it to go on forever. I hate his eyes on my body. I like his eyes on my body. Then why do I feel so guilty?

He walks around me and I stand motionless. He stops in front of me and raises my chin. He shakes his head, his mouth turned down in disappointment. I want nothing more than to make up for that disappointment but haven't a clue how. Is it me or the clothes?

He tilts his head and gives me a small smile. He is the type of person whose smile transforms him. My breath catches in my throat. He raises his hands to my hair. It is a little longer than shoulder length. "Maybe up," he muses. His fingers slide up my neck. Blood roars in my ears. I try not to sway on the incredibly high heels. I can feel my nipples thrusting their turgid way through the fabric. I'm sure they will spring out of the low dress at any moment. His fingers are lightly fooling with my hair, the wisps that escape and fall causing chills to ripple over my body. Has he turned off the air conditioning? My body is on fire. My breath fast and shallow. His hands are massaging my scalp and I feel my insides melt before beginning to form a hard ball of need. I close my eyes. My mouth becomes slack. A finger, an incredibly gentle finger slides down my neck and into my dress. My knees weaken and I sag. He pulls me upright and tilts me slightly backward by the back of my hair. My body is arching towards him. I feel his thigh between my legs. The finger is making small gentle circles on my nipple and I bite my lips. My hips begin to move. The wisp of material at my crotch does nothing to stop me from feeling the stiff, slightly scratchy feel of his pants. I'm already too far gone and I can't help but try to find my release. My body is now in control. A moan escapes me and then he pinches the hard nipple and I find myself coming and coming. I collapse against him, gushing and weak as his finger keeps up its relentless movement that is pleasurable pain.

Mister Caldwell tilts my chin up. My eyes are glazed. "You're a bad girl Miss Julia. Bad girls need to be corrected and shown the right way to act. But first bad girls need to be punished." His words don't penetrate my dazed mind. I feel his arm around my waist supporting me. He walks me to the couch and sits on it, dragging me across his lap. My face is on the cool black leather. I feel the satin brush up my bare cheeks and realize too late the position I'm in. My rear is raised higher because of his knees and naked thanks to the briefs. My mind begins to clear and I make a motion to rise, the swift stinging contact of his hand on my bare flesh shocking me into staying put. The sting penetrates and I clench my buttocks but not before another swift blow lands. His left arm holds me securely on his lap. The smacks are fast and furious, the heat building steadily. I whimper in confusion and pain and his left hand snakes under my belly and moves lower, seeking that hard little bud that betrays me. His thumb and forefinger keep time with his steadily falling hand and I find myself unable to distinguish between the two sensations. Both cause me to heat up but in different ways that seem oddly the same. Both lead me toward the same thing. I feel the heat centering low and them I'm screaming as I come and come. His right hand stops its attack and slowly, soothingly makes small light circles on my flaming rear.

I'm spent. Useless. Unable to move. He shifts his position and I'm on my back, legs obscenely straddling the wide couch. I look up and see his outline against the spotlights. I can't make out his features. He is a black silhouette against a white background. I hear the rasp of a zipper and then he's hovering above me. His hands take hold of the top of the dress and rip it apart in one easy motion. The wisp of panty follows. I feel his mouth on my breasts but I'm still too weak to respond. His hand is between my legs and then a pressure.

It intensifies and my mind finally clears but its too late. I gave a gasp of pain and try to tighten my legs against the invading shaft. "Lie still," he orders. I obey. He waits a few minutes and the uncomfortable feeling eases.

Then he fucks me. He makes no sound but a grunt at the end. I expect him to rise but he doesn't. He remains on top of me, his penis still inside of me. "Are you on the pill?"

I shake my head. He tells me he'll order them for me tomorrow. He takes my chin in his hand and kisses me lightly. "Now that this is out of the way, things will be even better."

I can't quite take in all that just happened. I'd always wondered what it would be like but never had I thought of it happening this way. Where were the loving kisses? Things happened differently in books and movies.

I see that disarming smile and continue to stare at him. I haven't uttered one word of protest. I haven't uttered one word.

"I'm sure the other clothes are appropriate for dinner with clients. This one was just for me." This one lay in shreds beneath me.

He shows me a door on the dark side of the room and it leads to a bathroom. The room is the direct opposite of the other room. All bright lights and white on white everything. I stare in amazement, squinting against the unexpected attack of light. Everywhere I look I see myself. Every wall is mirrored from floor to ceiling. I see a dazed woman staring back at me. She is naked with a small trickle of blood running slowly down the inside of one thigh. I stare at it stupidly. Slowly I see it for what it is and all I can think of is that if I don't clean myself it will stain the too white carpeting. I hear his words. 'Bad girls need to be punished,' and I hurry into the shower. The water snaps me out of my bewildered lethargy.

My boss has just raped me and here I am calmly showering in his bathroom. I let the warm water hit my skin. I turn the force up. I welcome the sting of the water, it keeps me awake. What is it that he has that I so blindly obey him? I turn and let the water pound my back. I slowly turn my head this way and that as if trying to work out kinks in the muscles. I turn and a jet of water hits a sensitized nipple and I flinch. It reminds me too much of his fingers squeezing it. The same kind of pain that brought so much pleasure.

I look down and see the gentle sloping of my belly. My fingers slowly, hesitantly explore between my legs. Virgin no more. Why don't I feel any different?

I wince as I hit a tender spot and drop my hands. It's hard to exactly recall the tumultuous highs I had felt not long before. Had I shamelessly used his thigh to achieve my pleasure? How would I ever face him again?

The door opens and he walks in naked. He has a very good body. My eyes widen in embarrassment and I immediately turn my back towards him. There is nowhere to hide in the clear glass shower stall. The door opens and I feel the sting of a slap on my backside. The surprise makes me turn. Probing eyes hold mine and once again I am lost in his gaze.

I watch helplessly as he soaps up his hands and then those slippery fingers are washing me. I turn to liquid. His hands move over my entire body, probing, caressing, arousing me to a fever pitch. "Open your legs."

I do and he teases the hard bud till I can barely suck in breath. Hands turn me and he pushes me forward. My breasts flatten against the warm glass. I feel fingers stroking my ass followed by another sharp slap. Heat builds hotter and then I feel a slippery finger inserted into my anus. I jerk with reaction but his hand on my neck keeps me against the glass.

"Please," I whimper.

"Please what?" he whispers in my ear, his finger easing in and out.

"I don't like it."

"But that's not important is it?" His voice is husky and echoes slightly. He keeps his finger moving and then withdraws it quickly. The hand still imprisons my neck. I am panting, my face turned sideways, my hands pressed against the slippery walls of the shower. I feel him shift sideways and feel four quick slaps on my backside, so quick I hardly have time to react and then he is behind me and easing into me. My sore cunt complains but I already know that for me to do so would be useless. I don't utter a sound.

I feel no pleasure this time and I instinctively know he didn't mean for me to. He pounds me viciously, more of what one would think an animal would do rather than a man. I hear his hushed grunt and feel him rest his forehead on my shoulder. "You've no idea how good a really tight cunt can feel," he murmurs to me and then I am released.

I lay against the glass until I hear the shower door close. The sound of a machine finally rouses me and I see him standing between two thin partitions. He catches my eye and holds my gaze. That wonderful grin that throws me completely stretches his lips and I find myself responding with my own shy smile. He winks at me and walks into the other room still naked. I can't take my eyes from his broad shoulders and muscular back. His tight ass doesn't wiggle like mine.

I continue to stand under the water, unaware of it. I feel suddenly deserted and sad. I want his company. I want his nearness. The thought frightens me a little but I refuse to listen to it. I hastily turn off the shower and step out. I can't locate any towels. My eyes turn to the thin partitions and I warily approach them. As soon as I step between them I am caressed with warm air. The gentle breeze lulls me into calmness as it dries me. I've never experienced such sensations. It's as if a hundred light fingers were patting me dry with cotton balls. I raise my arms and turn slowly. Delicious.

I enter the black room still naked. It is empty and I feel a quick flutter of panic. What if he'd left me here alone? I squint against the light and the panic balloons. I can't locate the door. The wall seems unbroken. I'm disoriented again and search the other walls frantically. I turn and move more into the blackness of the dark half of the room. I see the door into the bathroom and open it to reassure myself it is what I think it is. The light pours out and I see a cabinet against the dark wall. It is black and only the glint of the bathroom light on the knob had drawn my attention to it.

I leave the bathroom door open and approach the cabinet. Can a cabinet look sinister? I raise a hand to the knob and let it fall almost immediately. Do I want to know what is in there? I lift my hand again and I see it shaking. My heart is hammering in my chest. The knob is cool beneath my touch. I ease it open and stare in horrid fascination.

It only has two shelves inside but they are full of handcuffs, riding crops, whips and chains. A few magazines lay on the bottom shelf and I see pictures of girls tied in different positions on the covers. I can feel the blood leaving my face and I hold tightly onto the door to support myself. What am I doing here? My breath seems to get caught in my throat and I sway dizzily. I have to leave before it's too late.

I shut the door and the bathroom door. I'm sure I entered the room from the opposite side. Shaking fingers feel along the black wall. The wall isn't painted.

It has some type of covering on it. I push a finger against it and it gives slightly. It's padded. Like a cell. I swallow quickly and continue to run my fingertips over it and I finally feel the crease of an opening. I can't find a door knob. I raise my hand to pound on it but the pressure of my other hand on it makes the spring lock work and it glides open noiselessly. Instantly I feel foolish over my panic and his knowing smile as he watches my face makes me feel more so. I stand awkwardly in the doorway, embarrassed.

He turns and walks towards the couch where clothes are laid out in neat rows. "I'm sure all the undergarments will fit but lets try on one dress to be sure the measurements are accurate." He turns and beckons me impatiently forward. I hesitate and see the slightest trace of annoyance cross his features. "I'm waiting."

Say something, my mind screams but I do nothing but what he tells me. The dress in his hands is the softest of pinks. I stand before him and raise my arms, too aware of how close his lips are to my bare breasts. I feel the nipples tighten. He tosses the dress over my arms and tugs it down gently, a fingertip stroking the turgid tip as it passes. I suck in my breath as a white flash of heat sears through my body from my breast to my loins.

"Always remember that feeling," he says conversationally and then turns me so he can zipper me up. The dress hugs me sensuously, the soft brushed cotton stroking my skin as I move. He's looking at me critically and again I lose my confidence.

"It's very pretty," I murmur, suddenly afraid he'll take it back if he doesn't like it.

"It'll do," he answers. I turn for him to undo me and he does, a fingertip lightly trailing above the zipper sending chills down my spine. I'm disappointed when the zipper ends at the curve of my back.

He gathers the clothes together while I dress and

taking my arm we leave the building. His driver is waiting for us at the curb. "Miss Davis' hotel," he instructs and then ignores me and concentrates on some papers from his briefcase. I look out the window.

Why am I letting him do this to me? My hands clench each other nervously in my lap. My mind shifts. Did I make the bed this morning? Is the room neat and tidy? Why do I assume he'll come up to the room? He never has before.

He does.

I want to rush ahead and make sure all is neat but his hand is once more on my arm. Why is his grip always so tight? I fumble with the key and he takes it from me. The door opens and he waits for me to precede him. I stumble in, my first feeling one of relief that the bed is made and the room is straightened. I turn and see the look of distaste on his face as he looks around. My eyes suddenly see what was a comfortable room has become a shabby place. How had I never noticed the mended curtains, the rickety stand the television sits on. I see worn spots in the carpeting and blush as if it is my fault.

He catches my eyes and again I'm held. My breath shortens and I feel my scalp tighten. He smiles at me. It's a small smile. Why do I feel it's sinister somehow?

He approaches me and lightly rubs his hands up and down my arms, his fingertips brushing my nipples with each stroke. I immediately shift gears and my mouth goes slack. His hands stroke my neck. I close my eyes. I don't feel him unbutton my blouse. I'm not aware of it till the cool air brushes my skin. His hands stroke and caress me till I lose track of where they are and what they're doing. My breasts are freed from the restrictions of my bra. He is pushing my blouse off my shoulders, down my arms. I feel it fall, feel his hands holding my wrists behind me. He kisses me and I become a mass of sensation. His tongue works deep in my mouth. Seeking. Probing. I try to drink it in. He bites my neck lightly and then sucks one nipple into his mouth. I am arching back, trying to push even more breast into his mouth. He lightly bites the tip and I sag to my knees, weak with desire. It is then I realize my hands are tied behind my back with my bra.

I feel a flash of sickening fear. I'm frightened. I don't like the feeling of being so helpless. "Please," I whisper, my voice sounding ragged.

"Please what?" he whispers back. I see his hand going to his zipper.

I'm shaking my head back and forth. "I can't." My breath rushes from my body making my voice harsh.

"But you will." How can his voice be so casual?

I'm looking at his penis directly in front of me. I can't tear my eyes from it as I continue to shake my head. "I've never. I can't. I won't." I hear his sigh, see his hand start to undo his belt buckle and my mouth opens as if it has a mind of its own. He cups my chin with his right hand, his left knuckles brush over my lips. My insides become liquid heat. I feel the heat starting to center between my legs. He slips the hard shaft between my lips. It has a rubbery feeling and feels twice its size in the small confines of my mouth. I feel a tear slip down my cheek. I don't know what to do so I just keep my mouth open and let him rock back and forth inside of it. I gag each time he goes too far and hear him tell me to shush as if it were my fault. I try to think of other things. Try desperately to not think of what will happen when he shoots into my mouth. I feel his hands on the back of my head keeping it still. He pushes only the tip in and out and I feel the ridge against my lips. I hear his quick intake of breath and feel the spurt of hot liquid hit the back of my throat at the same time I hear his soft grunt. I take one more breath and then choke.

Fingers under my chin stop me from spitting it out. He doesn't say one word and after a long pause I steel myself and swallow. "Good girl," he murmurs, his hands slipping to my breasts where they stroke and caress. My nipples betray me as always. He lifts me to my feet and sucks a nipple into his mouth. His tongue swirls around and around and I have to clench my legs together. He leaves a wet trail from one to the other and I'm almost whimpering. I'll go crazy if I don't finish. His fingers rub my crotch through my skirt. It's a tight skirt and hugs my belly closely. I shamelessly push against his hand. He backs me up to the wall and holds me to it with a hand on my chest.

"Use my hand but do it yourself," he orders. I'm too far gone to stop, too far gone to feel embarrassment. I thrust my hips forward and ride his hand, almost crying with frustration as the feelings build and build. He stops and pulls me off the wall and throws me across the bed. His hand thrusts up my skirt and I open my legs as far as my skirt allows. He grabs my clitoris and rubs it hard. I'm beside myself in a frenzy of lust. I feel the sting of his belt across my rear at the same moment he pinches my engorged bud and I ride the waves of painful ecstasy until they slowly ebb and my heart begins to beat at a near normal rate.

I feel him loosening my bonds. "Never say won't to me again Miss Julia." The bra drops on the bed in front of my eyes. "Don't be late for work."

He's gone. I lay spent across the bed, my arms limp and weak by my sides. Why am I letting him treat me like this? Am I so desperate for love I'll accept any kind? Am I so lonely I'll put up with anything just not to be alone?

I turn over and lay staring at the ceiling. My hand

rises of its own volition to my breast. I caress myself languidly. I've always liked being stroked. My mother used to sit out on the front porch with me curled up at her side and read to me. I'd snuggle against her breast and look at the pictures in the book, enjoying the lazy, unconscious way her arm around me would stroke my back and arm. It always made me feel so safe. At night she would lovingly brush my hair for me and I'd melt under the light tug of the brush, the feel of the bristles against my scalp heavenly.

I hear a television go on in the next room and it rouses me. I'm still sprawled on the bed half naked. I sit up and notice for the first time a gold bangle bracelet on my right wrist. It's beautiful and a sense of happiness settles deep in my stomach. He's bought me a gift.

It's oval shaped and fits my wrist snugly. Actually there's no space except for the two ends. The top and bottom are almost flush with my skin. I study it and cannot find a catch of any sort to remove it. I run my finger over the metal but just like his door in the black room, this seems to have no seam. I spend a half hour studying it but still find no way to remove it. An uneasiness pushes the happiness aside.

It's not a bangle. It's a slave band.

I lose the argument I have with myself all Sunday night and find myself in my office Monday morning. I'm wearing a dress of navy blue satin. It's low cut but not too daring. The fabric hugs my body all the way to the hem. It if had reached my ankles it would have prevented me from walking. I walked in the too high heels all night trying to learn to do it properly. They pushed me so high I felt like I was mincing along instead of walking. I left them off and have my comfortable two inch heels on.

The morning passes and I don't see Mister Caldwell. He doesn't look into the room and I have no reason to leave it. I find it hard to concentrate. Is he at his desk? Did he come in today?

I look around the walls of my office and the space seems to grow smaller. I feel surrounded, trapped. My eyes linger on the doorknob. What excuse could I use? I stand suddenly unable to stay in the confined space any longer. I can feel pricks of panic starting to race up my spine. I don't even take a step and the door opens.

Knowing eyes look into mine. How does he always know? Does he have a hidden camera? My eyes flick around the room, searching. I see the amused smile that settles on his mouth. He knows what I'm doing. His eyes take in my appearance. I see the flicker of annoyance.

"Why aren't you wearing the matching shoes?"

"I can't walk in them properly." It sounds lame even to my ears.

"How will you learn unless you wear them?" I stare at him mutely. He approaches me and lifts his hands to my neck, stroking it lightly with his fingers. I shift from foot to foot as I fight the lassitude that threatens to engulf me.

"There is so much you have to learn Miss Julia," he whispers. The fingers continue their caress and he lightly kisses me. My breathing is becoming tortured. "You want me to teach you don't you Miss Julia?"

I nod. At the moment I would have agreed to anything. His fingers slip to my breasts and then he's gone and I'm standing beside my desk swaying. I open my eyes in disbelief. I need him. How could he leave me like this? Tears of frustration prick my lids but I haven't the courage to open the door. What would I say? I want to come. I want you to fuck me. I need you.

I sit down and clench my legs. My fingers itch to dive between my legs but I daren't. I'd die of embarrassment if he walked in on me. I try hard to concentrate on my work but it's almost impossible. Time drags.

I leave at lunchtime but he's not at his desk. I'm torn between two emotions. I want to see him but I don't. I'm afraid he'll read my mind again. I hurry outside and hail a cab. It isn't till I reach my room that I realize he never gave me my key back. I seek out the desk clerk and he lets me in, informing me there will be a twenty dollar charge to replace the key. I mumble I think I know where I left it. He gives me a disbelieving look and I shut the door behind him. I don't have much time.

The matching blue shoes are on the bed, not in the closet. I feel a moments panic that someone is in the room with me but a quick look in the bathroom assures me I am alone. The closet. I look at the closed door and am terrified of opening it. My palms start to sweat. My hand is on the knob but it still won't make the movement required to open the door. I am wrapped in fearful anticipation. I swallow hard and yank the door open, stepping back at the same time.

All my clothes are gone but the ones he bought me. I can't take it in and stare at them as if I expect the others to appear. I rush to the bureau but drawer after drawer reveals nothing but silk and lace and satin. Gone are all the serviceable cotton and rayon. My nightgowns are gone but I find nothing to replace them. Pantyhose no longer exists but is replaced with box after box of sheer silk stockings. Again the all too familiar feelings. I hate it. I love it.

I glance at my watch and am startled at how fast the

time has flown. If I have trouble finding a cab I'll be late. The shoes catch my eye. I hesitate only for a moment and then toss the ones I'm wearing into the trash. I stumble out the door and make my awkward way to the street. The desk clerk gives me a speculative look. I see a smirk settle on his lips and wonder how much he knows.

I'm late. He glances meaningfully at his watch as I walk past his desk. I see his eyes flick to the heels. I almost make it into my office.

"Miss Julia." His voice is so low. My throat tightens imperceptively. I turn. He crooks a finger at me and I find myself walking towards him. I know what he intends. Why do I do as he says? He swivels his chair so he is facing me and I only stop when our knees touch. I can't look into his eyes but stare straight ahead.

His hands crawl up my legs. He clicks his tongue. "No pantyhose Miss Julia." He pulls it down and it bunches around my knees. I hear another click of his tongue. "Didn't you understand my meaning?" He's pulling my white cotton briefs down also. My dress is up, hung up on my hips. My mound is only inches from his lips. I can hardly hear him because the blood is roaring in my ears. I feel his hands on my buttocks, stroking, smoothing. He pulls me slightly closer and I feel his breath on my pubic hair. My knees start to shake. I would do anything to feel his mouth on me. Time is suspended as I wait breathlessly. I can't move. I'm terrified he'll stop touching me. The hands turn me and I'm leaning over his desk. I feel his tongue on my left cheek and then he smacks me hard three times. I just lean on his desk and do nothing. Waiting. Wanting him more than I ever have.

I feel my clothes lowered, the tugging at the tangle at my knees. "Step out." I do and he pulls off my underwear and tosses it in the trash.

I straighten and finally meet his eyes. His gaze challenges me. I swallow. "But. . . ."

He's shaking his head slowly. "No buts. You have much to learn Miss Julia."

"Why do you call me Miss Julia?"

He ignores the question. I am standing directly in front of him still. His hands glide up my legs and stroke the soft insides of my thighs. I try to open them farther but the dress prohibits it. He comes to within an inch of my love canal but stops. His finger slides back and forth. I want it to go up and down. I can barely breathe.

"Do you like your bracelet?"

I nod wordlessly, barely able to concentrate on his words. "Every time you look at it I want you to remember what you are. You are a blank page that needs to be written on. You are a woman that needs to be shown how to give pleasure. You are mine to teach." His fingers move higher and start a mind dizzying circling. "I will show you many ways to have pleasure Miss Julia. There are infinite ways to give and receive pleasure just as there are infinite ways to give and receive pain. Each is much better when it's accompanied by the other. I will show you what you need to enjoy each."

His voice caresses me as if it is a soft warm wave that laves my body. I hear his words and don't hear his words. His fingers are doing a new dance and my body responds to each new movement. I would have let him plunge a knife into my breast as long as he didn't finish the dance too quickly. My body bursts into a thousand fragments and I sag to my knees. He pulls my dress above my hips as I rest my head on his knees. "We don't want to stain anything so pretty do we?" he asks, his fingers gentle and soothing in my hair.

The next week was the turning point in my life. I went to work each day and each day it was harder to concentrate on my tasks. Mister Caldwell would enter my little office two, three times a day and standing behind me he would look over my work. He never spoke but his hands were always, almost absently stroking my neck, my back. They would slip into the top of my dress and caress my breasts. So lightly. So delightfully. I was in a constant state of anticipation. He didn't touch me otherwise.

We have dinner with a trio of clients one night during the week. The oldest looks pointedly at my bracelet and speaks to Mister Caldwell in French. I feel myself blushing as they share a chuckle that seems potent with meaning. Mister Caldwell strokes my thigh under the table the entire night and I hear nothing of what is said.

Walking toward the limousine, the older client accompanies us and I feel a flash of uneasiness as my bosses hand tightens on my arm. The parking lot is only dimly lit. Sam the chauffeur gets out of the front seat to open the back door but Mister Caldwell stops him.

"I would like to see the notes from tonight's meeting," the older man says, his eyes steady, direct, challenging.

I blush. "I didn't take any," I stammer.

"Your secretary is a bad girl," he says to Mister Caldwell. I feel my boss turning me, his arm tight around my waist as he bends me over. I see the chauffeur's face watching with interest as I feel my dress sliding up.

"No." My voice is hardly above a whisper. I can't

stand the humiliation. Three men are looking at my bare rear. "No," I say louder. A hand covers my mouth and then I feel the sharp sting of a hand on my buttocks. I'm in a public parking lot being spanked like a recalcitrant child and the thought makes me struggle. The smacks get harder and then a hand cups me between the legs. The pain seems to diminish and be replaced by another feeling. The feeling grows and grows and I am shamelessly working my body against the probing hand. The hand leaves my mouth and I only pant, all thoughts of screaming for help gone. I feel the hard tubelike shape of a penis between my legs. It doesn't penetrate me but works its way back and forth between my thighs. I hear tortured breathing. Is it mine? Just as I begin to come I realize it is Mister Caldwell's arm still around my waist, his other on my neck holding me bent over. I see the chauffeur's smirk, see his hand lightly rubbing the front of his pants. I feel the stickiness dripping down my leg and then hear the murmured good nights from the elderly client. I can see him zippering himself as he walks towards his own limousine. I start to cry.

I'm bundled into the back of the car and handed a small wet towel. I clean myself and continue to cry. "Why?" I finally ask.

He turns my head and kisses me. Lightly. His lips move over my eyes, my lips, my cheeks. "Because I wanted to."

"You embarrassed me. Humiliated me." I sniff.

"Deep down you loved it. You need it Miss Julia. You need to be told. To be led." He puts his arm around my shoulders and his finger starts to caress my nipple. I hate myself for the instant response he gets from it. "I know what you need. Think about the feelings. Dwell on the feelings," he whispers.

I feel the need building again deep inside me and

then we're at the hotel. "Take Miss Davis to her door, Sam."

I don't want to go with the chauffeur but he is handing me out of the car. Like his employer his grip is tight and I have no choice but to let him lead me. I see the smirk on the clerk's face and feel my own flame. Sam waits for me to enter the room and then closes the door behind me. Mister Caldwell hadn't even said goodnight.

As I leave the office the next day he gives me a rare smile. It always throws me. "Wear your yellow dress tomorrow," he says and then goes back to his work.

On the way home I decide it's time to rebel. I won't wear the yellow dress. I'll choose what I'll wear. I am determined to stand up for myself until I open the closet door the next morning. In my mind I see the cabinet in the black room and what it holds. I put on the yellow dress.

It's a beautiful dress. It's soft, as are all the clothes he's bought me. Tiny buttons run from the very top to the very bottom. It has a wide tie belt in the same material as the dress. The skirt ends at my knees and flairs out slightly. It sways as I walk.

I work hard and the morning passes quickly. I haven't seen Mister Caldwell. Just before lunch the door opens and my heart starts to beat faster. He's smiling at me and suddenly I'm ridiculously happy. "Very pretty," he says, his hand raised for me to take.

I get up quickly and put my hand in his. He turns me this way and that. "I know what suits you," he says, the smile still on his face.

He lifts my left hand and I hear a low snap. I stare down at my wrist. I'm wearing another gold bracelet, a twin to the other. He reaches into his pocket and removes a thick short piece of chain which he clips onto each of the bracelets. I look down numbly. I seem to be wearing very fancy handcuffs.

"I finally decided what I want to hang from the other hook," he whispers from behind me. He raises my arms and lifts me off the floor. I glance up and see I'm suspended from the middle hook. I start to panic but my feet touch the floor and I feel a little better.

"Mister Caldwell?"

A piece of tape covers my mouth and now I do panic. My eyes are wide and I feel as if I can't pull enough air in through my nose. "Easy," he whispers, stroking my upraised arms. I feel him take the belt off and then I see nothing as it covers my eyes. "You'll have to trust me."

My breath is harsh. I am truly afraid for the first time. Images of the black cabinet fill my mind. I try to stand on tiptoe to loosen the chain so I can slip it off. I hear the clicking of his tongue and brace myself for a smack. Instead I feel my foot pulled sideways and I realize he's tying my feet to the legs of my desk. I can't move. I am stretched as far as I can be and still be able to support my weight. I feel his hands undoing my buttons. His fingers keep brushing my nipples and I feel my body shifting from panic to desire. He lightly caresses me between my legs and I feel myself sag. The pain in my wrists makes me straighten up quickly. Light fingers brush the two sides of my dress open and back. I'm completely exposed.

A finger strokes my neck and traces a light path down to my right nipple. It strums it gently. I moan and then I hear the door open. I don't hear it close. I strain my ears and hear the slight creaking sound his chair makes. I must be outlined perfectly in the doorway. Stretched. Virtually nude but for stockings and garters. The panties I wear are completely sheer.

I panic. Suppose Mrs. Porto enters his office. I strain

my ears. I hear low murmuring. Is he on the telephone? A voice answers. A voice with a French accent.

I feel myself go numb and I wait helplessly. Am I to be punished for something? I haven't done anything wrong. My arms start to ache, the muscles protesting. Time seems to crawl by. I'm filled with self-pity. I hear the creak of his chair. I strain my ears. I hear nothing. That damn thick carpeting.

A mouth touches my breast and sucks on the nipple. Lightly. Teasingly. I try to clench my legs together. I can't. Not a sound is made. A finger touches my engorged clitoris and I hear a gentle mocking laugh. Is it Mister Caldwell's?

Silence.

Nothing.

I'm starting to panic again. My heart is pounding. I'm straining to suck in air through my nose. I can feel a lump forming in my throat and it threatens to choke me. My arms are screaming.

The tape is pulled off my mouth and I gulp in air. A thumb brushes my lips and then enters. "Suck." I obey the whispered command. "Such a good girl deserves a treat."

He unties my feet and lifts me to release me from the hook. I'm still blindfolded and he grabs my hand when I raise it to undo the belt. I feel the chain unhooked from my bracelets. Hands stroke and knead my breasts. They rub and mold, caress and tease. My mouth opens and a tongue enters it. It probes and stabs into my mouth as if it was fucking me. It lowers to my breasts and I arch back, my hands behind me on my desk supporting me. My legs are nudged apart and I feel the mouth leave my breasts and the flick of a tongue caresses my mound. I almost swoon.

Then nothing.

I lean against the desk and wait for what seems like

hours. Nothing. No sound. I straighten and tentatively reach out a hand. Should I remove the blindfold? I hesitate. He hasn't told me to. Suppose he wants to punish me if I do? I sit there on the desk for the longest time and then finally pull the belt off my eyes. I'm alone. The door is closed.

I do up the buttons with shaky fingers and tie the belt around my waist. I'm at a complete loss of what to do. I glance at my watch. It's past my lunch hour. I'm not hungry. At least not for food.

I sit at the desk and stare at the papers. Figures and names blur together. I can only think of the feeling of a tongue on my breasts. I can't go on this way. I can't allow him to take me over so completely. I have to get away. How far would he expect me to go?

I stare at the gold bracelets and then frantically try to find the way to release them. I don't want to belong to anyone. I came to the city to be on my own. I have good skills and could get another job easily. I'm a hard worker.

My mind shifts gears. He said I deserved a treat. What would he consider a treat? Was it nothing more than a payoff for doing what he wanted? I didn't care. I wanted to know.

The day drags by and I finally collect my handbag from the bottom drawer and open the door. The Frenchman is still with Mister Caldwell. They both glance at me and smile. "Ah, the delightful Miss Julia," the older man murmurs, getting up and coming to me. He takes my hand and raises it to his lips. They seem to linger and I quickly snatch my hand away. I feel the blush suffuse my face. Had he been the one whose mouth I'd felt?

I mumble a hasty good bye and rush out the door. I barely nod at Mrs. Porto as I pass. Does she have any idea of what is going on? Am I the only one? Who was this Susan I replaced? Wouldn't she go along with Mister Caldwell? Why do I?

Mister Caldwell. Strange. I never realized before that I have no idea what his first name is. I have never heard it used or seen it on a name plate. Over the past few weeks I had come to learn how vast his company was. It occupies the top ten floors of the building. The receptionist, Mrs. Blake, Mrs. Porto, Mr. Caldwell and myself are the only ones who work on the top floor. I rarely have any reason to go to the other floors. My life seems to exist on the top floor and my room.

I wasn't home but a half hour when he let himself into my room. I come out of the bathroom, newly showered and almost have a heart attack when I see someone sitting on my bed. He just smiles that great smile.

"I've come to take you out to dinner and a show." No, would you like to go? Just a statement. I feel a pang of resentment that he is so sure I have no plans. I open my mouth to protest but he gets up and rummages in my bureau, removing stockings, panties, and matching garter belt. I watch him, the towel still clutched tight to my chest. Say something!

I don't. I merely move toward him when he beckons me forward. He takes the towel from me and dries me. I feel my skin respond to the light caress of the terry cloth. He lingers over my breasts, the feeling one of erotic delight. He dresses me as if I am a baby. His fingers are deft and sure. He handles the stockings as if it is something he does everyday. Does he? He hooks them to the garter belt and snaps one of the elastic straps. I draw a sharp breath and he kisses me lightly on the mouth. The sting recedes.

He chooses my dress, a slinky, sensual garment that is skin tight and daring. He slips the matching heels onto my feet, caressing each ankle as he does. He empties my handbag onto the bed and picks a few pieces which he puts in the small matching purse he takes from the closet. He brushes my hair and I melt under the steady, rhythmic fondling of the bristles. He looks into my eyes for a long steady moment and I desperately want him to kiss me. He doesn't.

He takes me into the bathroom and rummages in my makeup until he finds what he wants and then carefully makes up my eyes. I love every stroke. He kisses my lips lightly, puts on my lipstick, holds a tissue between my lips. "Close." I do. He throws the tissue away and takes my arm. I feel as if I am a fairy princess being whisked away by Prince Charming. As I pass the desk clerk it is I who smirk this time.

We go uptown to a restaurant he knows and likes. He orders the meal, the champagne, and the wine without consulting me. I don't know about such things so I don't care. We linger over the meal, the conversation light. He talks about his political beliefs. I haven't even voted yet so I listen and believe every word. He toasts my beauty and makes me blush with happiness. I see that crazy smile of his a few times that night and it never fails to throw me completely off balance.

The dinner over, we go to the theatre and I thrill to The Phantom of the Opera. The music is beautiful, the actors fantastic. During the intermission he leans towards me and caresses my cheek. I became locked in his gaze. No others exist.

"You know better than to fight your captor. Don't you Miss Julia?" His voice is so low. Almost husky. I stare at him mesmerized. I am almost panting as his finger continues to stroke and soothe. "She didn't know he could teach her wonderful things. She didn't know he knew what was best for her. But you do."

I can't break eye contact. I merely nod. I see his

smile again, feel his lips and know I am hopelessly in love and will do anything he wishes. I think he senses it too because he is strangely quiet for the rest of the evening.

We are finishing up the account I have been helping him work on and I begin to wonder what I will be doing after it is all tied up. I bring some papers into him to sign and tentatively ask.

He glances up at me and I see his brows raise thoughtfully. "Yes it will be time to go on to other things soon. There is much you still have to learn." I hesitate, not quite certain of his meaning. He sees it and hits me with his disarming smile. "I'll find something. Don't worry."

I do worry. I find that I am afraid it will be in some other part of the building and I won't see him so often. I redouble my efforts to do a good job.

He puts his head in the door just before five o'clock. "Plan to stay late." And then he's gone. I straighten my files. I file my nails. I shuffle and reshuffle papers. I check and recheck figures that I know are right. And I wait.

My watch says six thirty. My stomach growls. I fidget. My eyes search the corners of the tiny room. They linger on the bare hook. Memories wash over me and I can almost feel the tongue on my breasts. I close my eyes as that driving need centers low in my body.

I open my eyes and sit up straighter. Mister Caldwell has only made love to me twice. I think of all the times he has kept me in steady anticipation. Days. Weeks. How many times has he brought me to orgasm? I've lost count. Why?

The door opens and I start guiltily. His eyes narrow and I'm sure he knows my thoughts. "Come along."

I stumble to my feet, my face red. His hands takes my arm and he leads me towards the black room. I'm afraid. I pull back but he ignores it. He opens the door and again I'm disoriented. I think the couch is in a different position. I'm led to the high bolstered arm and bent over it. He clips my bracelets to a hook in each leg. I feel my ankles encased in leather then they're pulled apart and hooked to the same hooks. Blood rushes to my head. My heart is pounding. My mouth is dry. I realize the position he has me in. My stomach knots.

My skirt is worked up my legs. It snags on my hips and I hear his quiet curse. The next sound is of tearing cloth. "It's a shame," he says as if speaking to himself. "I really liked you in that skirt."

I feel the panic building. "Mister Caldwell," I manage to squeak out through a tight throat.

"Shut up." He says it so casually as if he were telling me good morning. His hands are stroking my buttocks. He leaves and I hear the door to the bathroom open. Light spills out and I find my eyes glued to the sinister cabinet. He comes back and shuts the door. I hear the whisper of a jar unscrewing. My blood is racing and I try to rear up. I feel his fingers pulling my cheeks apart.

"No. Please!" I desperately try to move. A greased finger jams into my anus and I squeal like a stuck pig. I begin blubbering. I hear myself promising anything if he'll stop. His finger is moving in and out. I feel no pain but am terrified of what he intends. I start to cry.

He pulls his finger from me and goes to the cabinet. I'm in complete panic. My hair is grabbed and my face lifted. I can hardly see out of my tearfilled eyes. "So much noise," he says sadly.

He jerks my head sharply and my mouth opens to protest. The leather gag is in place before I realize it. My protests sound like soft mewings. They have no substance.

I tense and clench my buttocks as tightly as I'm able. I hear his sigh. A sound hisses behind me and the riding crop cuts up underneath my cheeks. The pain sears through me and I'm struck speechless. Paralyzed by vicious surprise. He thrashes me fast and hard. Four. Five. Six times. I hear the tortured screams in my head but they only come out as wild moans through the gag. My bottom is on fire and I twist and turn as much as my bonds allow.

I feel his hard knob and then he ruthlessly enters me with a single thrust that seems to tear me asunder. He keeps going deeper and deeper till I think I'll pass out and then finally I feel his belly against my hot cheeks.

He stops and leans over me, brushing the hair from my face as I lay with my cheek against the leather seat. Tears leak from my eyes and I whimper. He unties the gag and I gulp in air, shuddering with pain. He kisses my cheek. My eye. "You make it hard on yourself Miss Julia. You must learn to trust me."

His voice is so low. Why does he always speak to me in such a low voice? They say if you want to get someone's attention, whisper. Is this what he does to me? Makes me calm down and quiet down so I can hear him. So I'll concentrate on what he says.

I take a shaky breath and he starts to move deep inside me as he kisses my neck. I don't dare move. He's impaled me on his shaft so deeply I'm afraid of being damaged. I lay quietly and let him do what he wants.

The pain lessens as times goes by. It's replaced by a full feeling tinged with something else. What? Not desire but what? I almost feel a perverse arousal. My clitoris enlarges but all feeling is centered in my anus. Nothing is there to manipulate the growing bud. He pushes deeply and I give a cry of alarm. I hear his soft chuckles and then he starts to move more quickly. Harder and faster. The arousal starts to lessen and the pain builds. Then his fingers are there where I want them and feelings shift once more. He palpates my vulva and then grabs the hard bud between forefinger and thumb. I am lost in a sea of feeling and I wiggle my ass. I like the feel of his bare skin against my buttocks. His belly is hard and I feel the hairs tickle my overly sensitive skin. I concentrate hard on achieving my release and I finally make it. I feel his member grow and then hear his distant grunt as I give myself up to nothing but the waves of pleasure that are coursing through me.

He kisses my neck, his hands under my chest, soothing, calming as my heart slows and my breath comes easier. I feel his breath in my ear. "Next time it will be easier."

He unhooks me from the couch and my head swims when I try to stand up. He laughs softly and holds me to him tenderly as my head clears. "Better now?"

I nod my head. I don't want to leave the safety of his arms. He holds me for another moment and then lifts my chin and brushes the damp hair from my forehead. He kisses my lips. I love him. He can be so tender.

I stand still when he starts to undress me. I watch him remove my clothes. He hands me the riding crop and I stare stupidly at it in my hand. "Put it away."

I do. I can't quite suppress the shudder that goes through me when I open the cabinet door. "Here."

I turn and he'd holding the leather gag out to me. I

take it and put it on the shelf. We shower. He dries me off and suddenly remembers I have no skirt to wear.

"You'll have to stay the night."

My belly twists. "Here?"

He quirks an eyebrow and I feel foolish. I try to stop the hammering of my heart. "Couldn't you get me a skirt from my room?"

He's putting on his jacket. I'm completely nude. "I won't have time tonight. I have an important meeting. I'll stop by on the way to work tomorrow."

My palms start to sweat. I'm hot and cold with fear. "I don't want to. . . ." I begin but he places his fingers over my lips silencing me.

"But I want you to." He takes my arm and leads me to the toilet. "Go to the bathroom. It'll be the last time tonight."

I'm shaking but I sit. My face flames as I hear the trickle of water leave me. I lower my eyes but his mocking laugh reaches me. He leaves and enters the black room. I have never felt so trapped in my life. I rise and wipe myself. I can't bring myself to walk into the other room. At least this room is bright and well lit.

"Miss Julia."

I shiver. I can't move. I'm paralyzed. He enters the room with an annoyed look and taking my arm jerks me forward. He pushes me onto the couch and flips me over so I'm on my stomach. My wrists are pulled forward and I hear the click of the clips. I'm bound to the couch, face down, hands attached to either side of the bolster. A hand on the small of my back. Another lightly smoothing my still warm rear end. "You have no idea how pretty pink stripes across your white rear look." He smacks me hard and I yelp. Again and again his hand comes down on my too sensitive rear. The pain centers and escalates. I am sucking in air between sobs. I start screaming but he doesn't stop. My buttocks are on fire and the fire is traveling down lower, creeping between my legs.

He kneels at my side and taps my lips. "Open." I do with a sob and he uses my mouth. He pulls out at the last minute and grabbing a handful of hair spurts all over my face. He leans down so his mouth is by my ear. "How long till you understand? How long till you realize how it is with me? You belong to me. You do as you're told."

He stands and shrugs back into his jacket. I don't move and he leaves the room. I lay staring at the two etchings on the wall. My body is screaming for release but I have no way to achieve it. My arms are wide spread, attached to each side of the bolster, and it prohibits me from trying to rise or move too much. I pass my first night in bondage.

He arrives early the next day with a change of clothes. I shower, dress and go to my office as if nothing has happened. Being tied to the couch all night has done something to me. I have a different perspective about everything. I no longer question his right to control me. I almost welcome it. I had struggled and fought my bonds till I was exhausted and then a sense of peace had descended on me. It was out of my hands. I want to do what he wants me to. What does he do? He makes my body come alive. I want to stay with him.

I finish my reports. I tidy my desk. I rearrange my filing cabinets and I wait for him to tell me what to do. He doesn't come in till five o'clock.

"We'll go for dinner." He waits as I collect my handbag and then takes my arm. I am used to the pressure he always uses and take it for granted. It is a way he has of controlling me. To others it only looks as if a solicitous man is helping a woman.

We ride down in the elevator. Whenever it stops he greets the workers who enter by name. He inquires after their health and that of their families. I am always amazed at his ability to remember so many people's names. He has that knack of putting people at ease right away. He is always concerned about personal problems and really listens when they talk to him. I stand mutely by his side and smile.

We dine at a restaurant not far from the building. The food is good, the wine delicious. His eyes keep catching mine and holding them. It seems he is probing for answers without asking questions. We finish and he asks for the check.

"We signed the deal today. Your work is finished." His words hit me like a physical blow. Is he letting me go? Is he telling me I am fired? I see him studying my expression. He has a curious glint in his eye. The bastard lets me suffer for a long moment as I try to gather my wits. "I have something else in mind."

Relief floods through me like a tidal wave. I am almost giddy with it. "Another account?"

"No. Something else."

He takes the check and signs it and then stands up. I follow his lead. He takes my arm and after bidding the Maitre D' a pleasant good night, we walk out and get into the limousine. He never says a word. I watch his face in the intermittent light thrown by the street lights. He turns and smiles at me and I feel better.

"Do you know I don't know your first name?" I ask with a smile.

His features never change. "That's right you don't."

He takes my hand and changes the subject. I hardly listen to his plans about closing the entire building for a two week holiday each summer. He isn't going to tell me his first name. Why?

A hand turns my chin towards him and he kisses me. His fingers smooth my hair back from my cheek as he lightly rubs noses with me. "I want you with me."

"I want to be with you."

"This is your decision. But it's one you must make tonight. There'll be no turning back either way."

His words cause me to pause. Run, my mind yells but his lips are nuzzling my neck and I stretch my head higher to make access to it easier. His fingers rub the material over my breasts and I begin to pant. I want him so bad. "If you stay with me you will do as you're told," he whispers, his lips playing over my eyes.

"Yes."

"Always."

"Yes."

His knuckle rubs up and down my thigh. I moan. He gives me another light kiss and then starts talking to Sam as if I wasn't there. I could scream in frustration.

The car stops and Sam opens the door. I am surprised to see we aren't at my hotel. Mister Caldwell says good night to Sam and leads me into a foyer. "Is this your apartment house?"

"Yes."

He uses a key for the elevator. The door closes behind us. "Am I staying the night?"

He gives me a funny look and pulls me close to him. His eyes are only an inch from mine. His tongue comes out and licks my lips, my eyes. I feel the cool air conditioned air turning them icy as soon as his warm wet tongue leaves.

"You're staying here for as long as I want you to." His tongue invades my mouth before I can utter a word. What did he say? Thoughts evaporate as his fingers lower my zipper. My dress slips and his tongue is licking my breasts. He teases the nipples, lightly tugging at one then the other with his lips. When the doors open, I am hardly aware of the rooms he walks me through. We stop at a door and he uses a key to open it. He urges me inside, and leads me to a beautiful bedroom. The bed is high and enormous with a beautiful brass headboard and footboard. I hardly see it.

I am helping him get me out of my clothes and out of his. I want him desperately. We fall onto the bed and he holds my arms down at my sides and makes slow passionate love to me for hours, taking me to the heights each time and then easing off till when he finally allows me to orgasm I almost pass out from the intensity. Just as I doze off I feel him pull my arm up and hear a muted click. I sleep the sleep of exhaustion.

I wake up alone and lay still for a few minutes taking in my new surroundings. I stretch luxuriously. He had been so tender, so loving last night. Nature calls and I try to rise but find my right wrist attached to a hook on the headboard. I rise to my knees but can't figure out the way to detach it. Like my bracelet it doesn't seem to have a way to unhook it. I feel a tingle of apprehension down my spine. Why has he tied me? I want to stay with him. I wouldn't have left.

I never heard him come near the bed. The sound of his voice startles me and I jump. "Problems?"

He is standing by the side of the bed in his suit.

"I can't get loose," I mumble, tugging ineffectually at the hook.

"It's made that way on purpose." A chill creeps down my spine. I try to smile.

"I'll be late for work."

"You're through working for me at the office. You'll serve me here from now on."

I turn incredulous eyes towards him. I feel the blood leave my face. Serve? "I don't understand?"

He takes the bracelet in his hand and does something because it detaches from the hook. "There's nothing to understand. You agreed to stay here and do what I ask."

"Yes but. . . ."

My chin is jerked up hard, my teeth catching my tongue between them. I cry out in pain but the pressure on my chin doesn't lessen. "No buts. I want you to stay in this room today. I'll show you where you may go when I have more time." He releases my chin. "The bathroom is through that door. Don't go anywhere else." He walks away from me and turns just as he reaches the door across from the bed. "You might be interested in what's in those two cabinets by the television."

Speechless, I watch him walk out and close the door. Was he telling me I was a prisoner? I rub my sore tongue over my lips. First things first. I enter the bathroom and take care of business. I see my toothbrush in the holder and opening the medicine cabinet I find all my toilet articles but my razor. I glance around curiously. It's a large bright colorful room. The walls are white but they are filled with colorful prints. My smile fades when I notice the hooks in the ceiling at various places around the room. There is an old fashioned tub, deep and long against one wall. Clips protrude out of the wall above the faucets. I check the shower stall and clips protrude along the back wall at various heights.

I have to get out of here. I leave the bathroom quickly and open the closet door. Nothing. It is completely empty. I feel the panic building. I rush to the bureaus and open the drawers frantically. Nothing. I stand in the middle of the room and my eyes search for anything I could use as clothing. There aren't even curtains on the high windows. My heart is beating a wild tattoo in my chest and I take a deep breath to keep myself in control. I run to the two cabinets by the television and yank open the doors simultaneously. I wish I hadn't. The top contained row after row of pornographic tapes. The bottom held a wider assortment of gadgets and whips than the cabinet in the black room.

I sink to my knees in horror. What have I agreed to? Why would the man who had made such passionate love to me last night need these things? I see another door and rise quickly. I have to get out! I grab the doorknob and find myself on my back an instant later. My hand is numb. My mind stunned and unable to function from the strength of the electric shock. The numbness leaves and the pain begins. I watch a blister form. The tears start and I lay on the thick rug and cry till I can't summon any more strength to continue. I crawl to the bed and collapse, exhausted.

He returns at lunch time. I have spent most of the morning pacing and fretting. Things like this don't happen in the heart of New York.

I don't hear him enter the room as I lay listlessly on the bed. I jump at the sound of his voice. He stands by the side of the bed and lifts a hand. "Let me see your hands Miss Julia."

Instinctively I curl my fingers inward to hide the blisters. He pries them open and shakes his head, his lips pursed as if in thought. "You've been bad again haven't you Miss Julia?" The very lack of emotion in his voice terrifies me.

He grabs my ankle and pulls me to the side of the bed, flipping me onto my stomach. I try to crawl up onto the bed but he twists one arm up behind my back and keeps me still. "I thought you understood better than you do Miss Julia. Haven't you realized that I am your master? Haven't you realized how it is with you yet?"

He clips my wrists together behind me. I lay panting on the bed, tears pouring from my eyes. My legs are strapped together with his belt and attached to the side bar. I hear him walk away and open the cabinet door. My tears come faster. I blubber and choke. "No. Please." I must whisper the same words a hundred times before he walks back towards me. I feel his fingers around my neck and hear a muted snap. I feel the thin piece of cold metal that surrounds my neck. He clips a snap onto it and pulls a length of attached chain forward till he affixes it to the other side bar. I lay helpless before him. Unable to move backward or forwards. He leans over my back and tickles my ear with his breath. "This lesson would have had to be learned sooner or later anyway Miss Julia."

He straightens and I tense, waiting. He makes me wait a long time. I hate the silence. I can't turn to look behind me.

A hand strokes my arms. My neck. My buttocks. Lightly, ever so lightly. It is soothing. Calming. My heart slows its wild race. His hand slips under me and he manipulates me for a moment. I feel my body shifting toward pleasure. The hand leaves.

I hear a soft hiss and then feel the cut of the cane he holds. It bites deeply into the soft fleshy part of my ass. The pain seems to hesitate for the briefest time and then starts radiating outward and inward. I clench my cheeks just before another blow falls. He thrashes me hard till I even lose the strength to scream. He throws the cane on the bed in front of my eyes. I hear nothing but my own moans and tortured breathing. The fires of hell couldn't be any hotter than my rear is at the moment.

Time passes and it slowly becomes a bearable throbbing. The touch of a hand on the too sensitive skin makes me suck in my breath. "Watching you squirm so deliciously has awakened my desire for you Miss Julia."

A hand between my leg, scooping up moisture. Feeling my cheeks pulled apart and the moisture applied. He gives me no leeway. His tool plows my tight tunnel with no thought of mercy. He thrusts himself deeply and I tense, gasping. He stops his vicious movements and leans down over my back. His lips caress my neck. His finger brushes the hair from my cheek.

"You're a natural whore aren't you Miss Julia? Even in your naivete you know how to pleasure a man." He blows lightly into my ear and nuzzles the lobe. "Tense your bottom again Miss Julia."

I do and whimper. "It hurts."

Lips nibble at my trembling lips. "I could ruin you completely in just a few minutes Miss Julia. Milk my rod and make me come with just your movements. Tense your bottom like the young whore you are. The sooner you pleasure me the sooner your ordeal ends."

He lays over me and I tentatively tense my sphincter. The soreness doesn't ease and my movements add to them. The touch of his belly hair feels like steel wool on my sensitive cheeks but I do as he says, tensing and easing, and even making small thrusting movements. My arms ache. My rear burns both inside and out but I keep going and finally after a long while I hear the distant grunt behind me.

His weight on me increases as he relaxes. "You have no idea how tight you are. You're almost virgin cunt doesn't hold a candle to your ass dear.'' He straightens and pulls out, the movement almost as painful as when he'd been buried in me. I watch him walk to the bathroom. I hear the water run. He comes out drying his hands a moment later. I can't help clenching my cheeks. I am disturbed by the lingering feelings of . . . what? Not desire. Not arousal. But something somewhere in the middle.

He unstraps my legs and unhooks the chain from the necklace. I lay still, unsure of what he wants. He strokes my hot cheeks lightly. ''Did you learn anything Miss Julia?''

I nod. ''I'll obey you sir.''

''Good girl.''

I feel my hands unclipped and slowly rise, rubbing my arms to get the circulation back. He slips an arm around my back and pulls me to him. ''Think of this while you wait for my return.'' The words are low and I strain to hear them. His finger is circling my left breast, his tongue is teasing my right. I swear there is a nerve that goes from each breast directly to my clitoris. Even as my rear still throbs, that incorrigible tiny organ begins throbbing to a different tune. I hold onto his head to keep upright as he works on my chest. His hair is as soft as I thought it would be.

Please touch me lower. Please, I scream silently. I am so close to coming and then he stops. He gives me a steady look and then a mocking smile. ''Remember the feeling,'' he whispers, picking me up and laying me on the bed. He raises my arms and attaches my wrists to the railings. Silken nooses slip over my ankles and stretch my legs wide and down before tightening. He flicks a finger over my nipple and an electric charge rushes to my loins.

''I wouldn't want you playing with yourself Miss Julia. That would be naughty.'' He leans down and kisses me, his tongue lightly licking my eyes, lips, the inside of my ear. His breath tickles me and I need to clench my legs tight but am unable. "Remember the feeling," he whispers and then leaves.

I lay stretched out naked on the bed. My body throbs with need. All thoughts of pain are long gone, replaced with a different kind of pain. A yearning pain. A needing pain. A frustrating pain. An exquisite pain. I have all afternoon to get to know it better.

I doze on and off, opening my eyes one time to find him staring down at me. It makes me feel more helpless that he can approach me so silently. He smiles at me and begins to gently knead my breasts. A finger trails downward, circling my belly button, tracing the light trail of down that descends to my pubic hair. My breath is harsh in my throat and I pant with sexual fever. His thumb presses my clitoris lightly and I whimper with need. He smiles again and releases me.

"Fill the bathtub all the way," he instructs and then walks out the door he came in by. I fight the need to rub myself as I hasten to do as he bid. I need for him to be kind to me. I need him to make me come.

I turn on the taps and pull the stopper up. The bath slowly fills and I turn to find him watching me from the door. He crooks a finger at me and when I approach him he attaches a small chain to my bracelets. Again I seem to be wearing pretty handcuffs. I see the thin gold necklace around my neck. He sees me looking at it and smiles. "You always see black leather wristlets and collars. I prefer the color of gold."

He helps me into the tub and then joins me. It is a huge affair and we both sit facing each other with plenty of room. He soaps the washcloth and starts with my face. His movements are slow and light and I feel myself relaxing, reveling in the feel of the slow circular movements. He lingers over my breasts and tantalizes me to near distraction as he cleans between my legs. He works on my feet and I find it oddly sensual. He sucks my big toe into his mouth and I have to hold my breath. He rinses me lovingly and I expect to wash him in return. I don't.

He rises from the tub and removes a board from the linen closet. He helps me out and places the board over the bottom half of the tub. It fits perfectly. "Lie down on it," he tells me. He steadies me as I step back into the tub. He turns me and tells me to sit on the edge. I do. I lean back and he raises my arms and attaches me to a hook in the wall. He steps into the tub and pulls me towards him till my rear end is almost hanging over the edge. My legs are spread over the sides and hang down. A noose tightens on each ankle and is attached to the feet of the tub. He settles back down into the water and proceeds to wash himself.

I am wide open and available to him for whatever he wants. He wrings the cloth out over my mound. The water teases and tickles as it trickles down through my pubic hair. I hear him splashing and then gasp as his tongue tickles my love bud. I try to move closer. I want to feel his whole mouth but I can do no more than wiggle up and down slightly. His bath goes on forever and all through it, I'm teased and tormented till I think I'll go insane with frustration. He takes his bath brush and pretends to comb the hair into different styles. Every time a bristle comes into contact with the tiny organ I feel a jolt of pure lust. He trickles water over it. He separates and spreads my vulva, palpating the hard knob now and then. His fingers dance around and in my vagina. A soapy finger rubs my anus and I feel a perverse arousal. His tongue, his wondrous tongue teases and licks. I can barely suck in breath. I'm going mad. Surely I'm going mad and then his whole mouth closes in on me and his lips are sucking the entire organ into his mouth. His tongue rolls it between his lips and I'm there, gushing, screaming, writhing in sheer bliss as the waves of relief wash over me. I'm limp.

I hear the water running. Feel steam caressing my body as he puts in more hot water. And then he starts all over. I will surely go mad. Just as I come again I hear his whisper. "See what good girls get."

I'm shaky on my feet when he finally releases me. I stumble into the bedroom, my wrists still attached to each other. I fall across the bed and let my heart slow down. He rouses me a moment later. "Miss Julia."

Slowly I open my eyes and turn my head to see him in the middle of the room. He crooks a finger at me and I stand up. "On your knees."

I have no strength to fight. I sink down. "Come to me," he whispers. I crawl to him. He bends and releases my wrists only to reattach them behind me. I am kneeling upright. I see his penis growing before my eyes. "You aren't a very good cocksucker, Miss Julia. You'll have your first lesson now."

I open my mouth and he enters. "Don't just let it happen. Make it happen," he tells me, his fingers twining in my hair, kneading my scalp as he moves me back and forth. "Suck it. That's a little better. Flick your tongue over the vent. Yes. That was good. Run your tongue down and up the length of the shaft. Yes. Better. Put more saliva on your tongue." He keeps stopping and prolonging the lesson till my mouth aches with being open so long.

"Start sucking it good now. Yes," he whispers, his fingers tightening on my scalp. "Be a good girl and swallow it all Miss Julia. You'll have to be punished if any messes the carpet."

I feel myself starting to gag as his grip hardens and his thrusting becomes deeper. Every time he hits the back of my throat, I fight not to retch. I feel the shaft swell slightly and then feel the spurts of thick liquid in the back of my throat. I force myself to swallow and then swallow again as another fills my mouth. He slows down and holds my head still, his pumping slower, easier. "Clean it," he orders and I do, licking the entire member till it's spotless.

He rubs my cheek and under my chin, his thumb brushing my lips. My mouth goes slack as my body instantly responds to his caress. "You're a good pupil Miss Julia. With enough practice you'll be as good as a pro."

He unclips the chain and I clean myself in the bathroom. He clips my left wrist to the headboard railing and then brings me a sandwich and watches me eat it. He takes the plate, turns me over, kisses me on my buttocks and then seeks his own bed.

There are pink welts on my rear end in the morning. He makes me wait to pee while he inspects them. "These will bruise beautifully," he murmurs.

He is dressed in a three piece suit when I come out of the bathroom. He sits on the bed and puts me over his lap. His fingers trace the stripes gently. His hand moves lower and all my thoughts center between my legs. He pushes his thumb into my anus. I can't help groaning. His forefinger finds my clitoris at the same time his other two fingers push into my vagina. In and out all his fingers go. I begin to work my hips but a quick slap to my rear stills me. I'm panting. I swallow and try hard to stay still but my body betrays me and again I begin to move with his fingers. He lets me this time. I grab onto the cover and hold tight to it as the feelings narrow and converge. "I didn't realize you liked feeling filled so much Miss Julia." I start to ascend that final level of tension and he stops. I push against his leg frantically but he pushes me off of him and I fall to the floor.

My hands instinctively seek to relieve myself and suddenly I'm pulled up and my hands are pulled behind me. "Naughty girl Miss Julia." I'm beside myself with the need to find release. He pulls me yelling and struggling to the cabinet. I'm so frantic I curse and swear. I beg and plead but he ignores my entreaties. My hands are clipped together behind me and then everything turns black as he slips a black leather blindfold over the top half of my head. I feel the laces tighten and the leather digs into my skin. I'm suddenly still. I hate not knowing. He picks me up and puts me over his shoulder as if I were a sack of grain. I hear the faint click of the lock on my door and then feel the hard bone of his shoulder digging into my belly as he carries me somewhere. He pauses and I hear a slight whoosh as if something is dragged across carpeting. We move. I hear it again. Another door?

He puts me on my feet and I stand still. I hear nothing and am terrified of falling. Suppose I'm by the open elevator door? Hands grab me and pull me forward. I'm babbling apologies left and right. Silence. My thighs hit something solid and I feel two thick straps separate and pin them to the solid object. I'm pushed down and I bend, another strap circling my waist and pinning me tight to what feels like a beam. It digs into my breasts that bulge sideways as they flatten against it. My hands are unclipped and pulled forward till my shoulders strain.

I hear the snick of the clip as I'm attached to something at full stretch. I'm whimpering and whining till my nose is held and I open my mouth for air. A round object is pushed in my mouth and tied at the back of my head. I remember seeing a leather ball gag in the closet.

I wish he'd say something. I'm sure I'm going to choke and frantically swallow around the ball. My breathing is tortured. Everything shifts the next minute as a tongue curls around my clit. My lips are spread and the tongue flicks in and out of my vaginal crevice. It takes long sweeps from the back to the front and my insides are melting. I curl my toes in exquisite agony. The tongue is relentless and I feel my thighs tensing. "Remember the feeling," he whispers and then shoves a slightly greased dildo into my ass. I strain against the agony but I can't move. I feel him attach it to the leather band around my waist. "Remember the feeling," he whispers into my ear and then rolls my engorged bud between thumb and forefinger. I tense, a scream sounds in the back of my throat and then I'm coming in gushes. I can feel the dildo moving slightly in and out as the pulses of my orgasm rock my body.

I hear no other sound so I assume he left for work. I try hard not to dwell on the large object that distends and fills my rear. I try hard not to dwell on the ball that distends my mouth and threatens to choke me. I dwell on what's happening to me.

I have become a sex slave for my boss. A flash of morbid excitement sweeps through my body. I have never liked pain. Have never sought it and yet when he beats me the pain builds and then fuses with arousal to an intensity that is overwhelming.

Remember the feeling.

I do. I love it. I love how his hands mold my body and take it out of itself. I am like a fine old violin in a master's hand. He causes my senses to tighten and hum, his fingers and tongue setting up vibrations that build and tremble till they reach a crescendo of feeling that bursts and slowly fades. But the master is able to play the same tune over and over and the instrument has no ability to deny his manipulations. I am becoming that violin. I am that violin.

I resent his power over me and my feelings. I love it. I resent how he'd tricked me by using my senses into agreeing to come here. I am glad he did. I don't like being so manipulated. I revel in it. I am an eighteen year old girl that is being trained to lead a life I had never known existed.

A few years ago my girlfriend Debbie and I had found a book called, Nine and a half weeks, in her brothers closet when we were looking for an old mitt to borrow. We'd started skimming through it right there and then, becoming in turn titillated, appalled, shocked and excited. So engrossed we'd lost track of time we didn't tear our eyes away from it till we heard the bedroom door close. Debbie's seventeen year old brother was leaning against the closed door, an amused grin on his face.

"Got ya," he whispered.

We'd blushed and stammered, hastily putting the book back but he still leaned against the door. He was looking at his sister's flushed face questioningly, thoughtfully. Debbie took a step backwards stammering, "You let us out of here or I'll tell Ma."

He'd snorted and advanced on us quickly, grabbing each of our arms. He pulled Debbie real close to his face. "I'll tell her it's yours." I saw her pale, sweat forming above her lip. "Mark please," she begged, her voice hardly a whisper. What had she been so afraid of?

He smirked and let her arm go, pushing her into the closet and shutting the door. I remembered the strange calculating look he gave me. His fingers had tightened and I tried to pull away. He pulled me closer and closed his other hand around my young breast. I gasped, half in shock, half in pain as his fingers tightened on the nipple. ''Be quiet,'' he hissed, his fingers digging into the soft flesh.

Debbie had made no move to come out of the closet and help me and I didn't know what to do. I remember starting to cry. I'd had no idea what to do. ''Debbie?'' I called but he hissed to shut up and continued to maul me. I started crying harder and he snorted with disgust. His hand snaked into my shorts and he'd swiped my slit before I could react. He let me go so suddenly I'd fallen and he'd stood there looking down at me. He showed me moist fingers. ''You loved it and you know it,'' he'd said quietly.

He opened the door and pulled his sister from it. I remember he never took his eyes from her terrified ones as he spoke to me. ''You get home and keep your mouth shut. Debbie and I have things to discuss.''

Debbie said nothing so I hurriedly left. She'd been distant to me after that. Would never talk to me about it or what had happened afterwards. My parents had died soon after and I lost contact with her when I'd moved to my aunts. I felt pretty sure now I know what was happening. Her brother had had some kind of horrible hold on her and it probably grew worse as she got older.

Something touches the inside of my leg and I tense. It is light. Almost as if a fly is crawling up my skin. I try to shake my leg but can't. It keeps going higher. I start to panic and then feel a thin rod moving back and forth over my vulva. It nudges my clit. It prods the dildo making me groan. I can't hear a sound. I can't see. I can't stand it. I whimper and feel a slash across my upper thighs. Everything in my body tightens against the pain. I make no noise. I hardly breathe.

I feel fingers on my clit. They make tiny circles. I don't know how but I stay quiet. One probes my vagina and rubs the inside of its tunnel. I feel the lubrication starting to ooze. Back to the engorged bud. I groan and feel another sting on my thighs. I clench the leather ball tight between my teeth. Fingers run lightly up and down the insides of my thighs. My insides are melting. A hand comes down on one cheek. I stifle my protest. I feel the hard tube of a man penetrate me from behind, his belly pushing the dildo deeper. He grinds into me, pushing and shoving, the pain in my backside taking over the thrill in my loins. The two feelings merge, divide, one stronger than the other and then changing. They seem to melt together and grow and grow and then I am screaming into the gag, a hand is smacking my rear hard and I feel the pulsations of fulfillment coursing through me. I whimper and cry with relief.

Silence.

I am alone again. Aren't I?

I actually doze. It's unbelievable what the human body adapts to. I come alert when the dildo is abruptly pulled from my body, giving a cry of fright as my thoughts fly in all directions. My anus pulses and throbs. Not with pain but with a strange sensation I can't quite name. A hand between my legs and then a clicking tongue.

"You've been a naughty girl Miss Julia. How did

you manage to excite yourself so thoroughly while strapped down. You need to learn better manners."

I can't believe what he is saying. It was him who. . . . . .wasn't it? I mew into the gag but I hear the swish and feel the sting. It isn't the riding crop this time. It feels like a paddle. A wide paddle. He gives me five hard smacks in quick succession and then releases the strap on my legs. I twist and turn my feet, digging one knee into the back of the other trying to alleviate the pain. It stings worse than the thin rod.

My bonds are loosed and I am led back to what I hope is my bedroom. I itch to take off the blindfold and gag but don't dare. He releases my arm and I stand still. I hate this feeling of helplessness. I only know I stand on thick carpeting. My hands are clipped behind me again and I stand there for long minutes. I can feel the moisture between my legs and panic thinking it might drip onto the carpet. I tense my thighs together and wait. My legs are tired and I want to sit but then I might stain the floor. I can feel the pulse in my neck beating rapidly as my heart quickens.

His voice is soft and low directly behind me. "You're learning Miss Julia."

The gag loosens and the hood comes off. I am back in my bedroom. Funny how what was a prison has become a refuge. He clips the bracelets in front of me and holds out the gag, mask and a large paddle. "Put them away." I do.

He goes into the bathroom and I hear the shower start. He comes back into the room a moment later nude. He does have a very nice body. He crooks a finger at me and I go up to him. He kisses my neck and shoulders. "Stiff?"

"MMmmm."

"The heat will loosen those muscles." He leads me into the shower stall. It's large and could easily fit four people. He attaches me so I'm facing the back wall. He adjusts the jets, there are four, and hot, almost too hot, water pulsates against my shoulders and lower back. I tense against the pressure but it only takes a minute till the water does its work and I feel my muscles loosening. I lean happily against the wall, small rivulets of water running down around my face and body. I breathe in the steam, the warm humid air almost sultry. My body relaxes further and I sigh. Vapor enfolds me, caressing me. I move my legs further apart and lean away from the wall slightly. The warmth wraps around me like a security blanket. Warm. Comforting. Safe.

Hands massage my shoulders and I lean back against Mister Caldwell. His fingers work and probe, easing kinks and sore muscles. He soaps them and washes my neck, my shoulders, my armpits. I'm in heaven. His hands move easily over my body, massaging, molding, exploring. He unhooks me and turns me. Refastens me tighter. His hands soap my belly, my buttocks, the crease between. They delve between my legs and caress, massage, soap.

"Lean back against the wall and don't move," he whispers. I open dreamy eyes. He holds a razor. The water seems to have turned suddenly cold.

"No. Please. Please don't do that. I don't want you to," I wail quietly, his steady hands already working the razor over my mound. I watch helplessly as the water catches the razor at the end of each stroke and carries the hair down to the tile then down the drain. My tears mingle freely with the water.

"Open."

I do. He's concentrating and careful. I'm not knicked once. "I'll redo it every two days to keep it nice," he says straightening. he looks into my eyes and gives me that lopsided grin that always shakes my equilibrium.

"Why?"

He kisses my lips lightly. "Because I wanted to."

I step out when he releases me and look at myself in the mirror. I look like a ten year old with boobs. I bite my lips and feel the tears forming. He chucks me under the chin. "Enough. No more nonsense."

I swallow and follow him between the partition to get dry. I feel myself blush every time he glances down at my pubis.

I follow him into the bedroom and watch him put on a terry cloth robe. It ties and comes to his knees. He even looks great in a robe.

"Nudity is wonderful at the right time," he says unexpectedly, "but I find a contrast more tantalizing." I watch him leave the room, hear the quiet snick of the lock and look at my hands in surprise. He hasn't attached me to anything. Not even my other hand. I feel awkward and can't seem to think of anything to do with them so I put them under my armpits. I drop them when he walks back into the room.

"I want you to wear this tonight." It's a black lace corset and thigh high black stockings. "Turn around."

I do and he puts the boned garment around my waist. I feel his fingers working the laces and then my breath leaves in a whoosh as he pulls them tight. "Get used to it," he warns and then pulls tighter.

I can't breathe. I'm going to suffocate. I glance down. My breasts are bare. It stops just below each breast and ends just where my pubic hair would have started. The back is higher and my rear is completely bare. He gives it one more tug and I grunt. He turns me and looks at me critically. "Not bad."

He kneels and picks up a foot, I grab his head to stay standing. I feel the silk ease up first one leg and then the other. I wonder how they'll stay up with no garter belt but he slides two elastic black lace garters up to the top of each stocking. They are stitched with tiny delicate rosebuds. High heels next and he stands and surveys his handiwork. "Not bad at all," he murmurs with a small smile. "Walk across the room."

I do, too conscious of my bare red ass jutting out behind me. I turn and it's worse. I can't get used to being hairless. I don't feel as if it's me anymore.

He nods his head in encouragement and devastates me with his smile. "Hungry?"

"Starving." I smile, happy he's happy. He opens the door and ushers me out in front of him.

The apartment is large. Very large. The living room is immense, filled with very modern furniture in black and white. One outstanding mural on a far wall lends the only color to the room. I see a dining area off to the left. Mister Caldwell takes my arm and leads me through a short hallway and then we enter the kitchen. It could be used to serve hundreds. He tells me to sit and attaches my left wrist to the chair leg. I watch him rummage in the refrigerator and bring out two pre-made dinners in casserole dishes. He pops them into the microwave and starts them heating. He takes a bottle of wine from the wine rack and uncorks it. I watch him move so confidently around the room and can't help wondering about him.

My thoughts don't even get started before he's talking. "I have a woman coming tomorrow to show you how to do your hair. I fancy the old pompadour style."

"No one wears that any longer Mister Caldwell," I inform him quietly.

"You will," he states and proceeds to pour the wine. He leaves the room carrying two glasses and returns just as the buzzer on the microwave beeps. I sit and watch him, pot holders on hands as he places the dishes on a tray and leaves with them. My hand creeps up to my hair. I don't think it's long enough for a pompadour but I wouldn't risk arguing with him.

He breezes into the room, takes a last glance around and then releases me. Hand on arm, he leads me to the dining room where we sit at one end of a table meant for thirty. It is in direct contrast to the living room. All heavy old furniture and Victorian print paper. The carpet is a deep burgundy red and as thick as the rest throughout the house.

He is very formal, seating me and pushing in my chair. The only thing that spoils the romance is when he clips my left hand to the chair leg. I have just enough leeway to rest it in my lap. He smiles and lifts his glass.

"You look lovely," he says with a smile and my heart skips a beat.

"Thank you," I murmur. Can this really be happening?

The casserole is chicken and mushrooms over rice pilaf. The sauce is tangy and rich and I find I'm truly starving after the first few bites. "Drink your wine."

"I don't care for it."

"Time to start. Take a sip."

I put my fork down and lift the glass. The aroma is heady and I hesitate but his steady gaze unnerves me and I do as I'm told. I wrinkle my nose in distaste and he snorts. "It's expensive wine. You'll have to develop a taste for it."

"Do you entertain a lot?"

He gives me a funny suspicious look and I hasten to add. "Having such a large apartment and such a big table I just thought," I give an apologetic shrug of my shoulders as my voice fades into silence.

"I give frequent parties. When you are more accustomed to my ways you'll sometimes join them."

I nod, not at all sure I'm happy with the thought. I

hear a muted bell ring twice and he rises and pushes a button. A moment later I hear a sound from the other room and we hear Sam's voice in the living room.

"In the dining room Sam." I feel the blood leave my face and try to rise, the bracelet keeping me in my seat. He must see the panic in my eyes for he chuckles softly at my embarrassment. "Get used to it pet."

Sam enters, his stride faltering for only a fraction of a second. I feel the blood rush to my cheeks and can't lift my eyes. I wish I could faint. Blood roars in my ears as he comes nearer. Wine is pushed under my nose. "Take a sip."

I do automatically, choking and spluttering as it goes down too quickly. Mister Caldwell pats my back for a moment and I catch my breath. "Take more."

I shake my head. The glass is under my nose again. I hear it clink against my teeth, feel the burning liquid slide down my throat. I'm told to keep eating and then I'm ignored as Mister Caldwell gives Sam his orders for the next day.

The food has lost its appeal. Is this the type of thing I'm expected to get used to? I push the food around in the dish and am told to eat and finish my wine. I nod without thinking and numbly put forkful after forkful into my mouth. It could have been sawdust. I drain the glass and don't taste it. Mister Caldwell gets up and releases me and leads me to a plush couch. He pushes me down gently and fastens me to the arm. A television comes out of the wall at the push of a button and I sit through the entire hour of news without hearing a word.

The sudden silence in the room brings me back and I find him watching me quizzically. "What is the big deal Miss Julia?"

I feel my face flame as his eyes lower once more and can't seem to utter a sound. He moves close to me and strokes my neck. His hands move to my breasts and in seconds I want him desperately. My thighs tense and clench in anticipation. His tongue licks and tickles my left nipple and my right one screams for attention. He works his lips down the lacy front of the corset. I feel his warm breath through the fabric when he exhales. Every nerve end is sensitized, anticipating. He pulls me flat on the couch and crouches between my legs. I feel his breath on my naked mound. A tongue. A kiss. A long swipe. I can barely breathe. My heart is hammering, my body on a roller coaster ride that takes me closer to the top with each touch. He rises and leaves me spraddled on the couch, my hips working.

"Please?" Tears leak from my eyes.

He turns back to me, looking down at me. "Please what?"

"Please don't stop." I'm almost whimpering with need.

He kneels at the side of the couch and sucks voraciously on my breast. My free hand is holding his head to my breast. He lifts his head, his eyes intense, inches from mine. "Don't stop what?"

"Please."

"Say it Miss Julia," he whispers. His eyes narrow as he watches me. "Say it."

"Please make me come." My breath is ragged, hoarse as the words squeak out of a constricted throat.

"Kneel over the arm."

I'm past caring and hurry to do his bidding. I kneel on the seat, my attached hand helping me to stay forward over the arm. My bottom is raised. I spread my legs. I support myself on the floor with my unattached arm. I wait.

I feel his hand pat and stroke my cheeks. His fingers explore my naked snatch, probing, manipulating but never touching the bud waiting to burst. I feel his tongue tracing the welts from my caning. I hold my breath as he makes his way lower to where my legs meet. I'm poised on the edge of a precipice, tottering, ready to fall, wanting to make the leap and then everything shifts and he smacks me hard and quick, the fire leaping from the contact of skin on skin right to the place I need it the most. I feel the lightest touch of a finger as he pounds me and I'm lost, screaming in painful ecstasy.

He pulls me back up on the couch and across his lap. I hear his own harsh breath as mine slackens. "I told you I knew what you needed Miss Julia," he whispers, opening his robe and slipping his penis between my thighs. I feel his hands on my hot rear as he works his shaft up and down against the new skin of my shaved mound. "It is so soft," he murmurs before I hear the now familiar distant grunt.

He keeps my lying over his legs, his now soft, still sticky penis crushed against my mound. I lay there quietly while we watch some old reruns on television. Every time he laughs I can feel the vibrations against my pelvis. His hand absently strokes my cheeks and the tops of my thighs, but I can tell it's a distracted touch, not one trying to arouse me.

He takes me to my room and the loosening of the corset is an immense relief. He watches me shower and then attaches me to the headboard. He smiles down at me and gently runs a finger along my cheeks. I feel his tender kiss on my brow and turning I fall into a deep sleep.

I'm awoken early the next morning. He seems impatient and excited which makes me very uneasy. I'm rushed through my morning ablutions and hastily dressed in a red satin corset with matching stocking and shoes. The garters are again black with red rosebuds. He takes me to the dining room, attaches the bracelet and comes back a minute later with eggs, bacon, juice and coffee.

"I don't care for coffee Mister Caldwell. Could I have tea?" I see his scowl and bite my lip but he rises and returns shortly with tea. I smile my thanks but he ignores me.

He eats quickly and I try to follow suit. A muted bell rings twice and he releases me and takes me back to my bedroom. He doesn't reattach the chain but stares at me deeply for a short time. "The lady to do your hair is here."

I nod, my mouth suddenly cry. Could I somehow ask for help? Do I want to? He tells me to sit on the bed and I do. I watch him open the door and call her to us when we hear the elevator door open. She enters like a small whirlwind.

"Mister Caldwell? Ida Crane," she offers at his nod. Bright alert eyes land on me. I see the eyes widen in surprise at my attire and hastily try to cover myself with the sheet.

Mister Caldwell pulls it out of my fingers. "Don't be ridiculous sweetheart. Mrs. Crane has seen naked women before." He turns to the older woman. "She was getting ready to try on her dress for the party. If you could just teach her how to get her hair right."

"Of course. I understand," the woman says quickly and then begins assessing my hair. "It is a might short. Women all wore their hair long then." She has me stand up and walks around me. "I think we can do it though. Take off those heels so I can reach your head," she says with a self deprecating laugh at her diminutive size.

I slip the heels off and stand quietly in front of her.

I can see Mister Caldwell watching me steadily. He cracks a grin and my heart flutters.

I'm taught to brush and manipulate my hair so it ends up in the eighteen hundred style pompadour. Mister Caldwell insists on trying also and I have a hard time keeping calm as his fingers stroke and caress my scalp and neck as he tries to arrange the hair. He's finally satisfied and ushers the woman out. Only when I hear the snick of the lock as the door closes behind them do I realize I might have lost the one chance I had of getting help. I still don't know if I really want to be helped.

We have dinner in the dining room, me dressed in corset, stockings and garters. My hair is up, a few curled tendrils hanging down. My eyes are made up just slightly darker than usual. The room glows with candlelight. I sit with my left wrist attached to the chair. The food is delicious.

Mister Caldwell is expansive tonight, talking about different topics, holding my interest with his light witty conversation. I find myself laughing and enjoying his wit.

"You're exceptionally pretty when you laugh Miss Julia," he compliments me, my heart starting to beat faster until he continues. "Yet I find I like it better when I see that look of fearful anticipation."

He reaches across the table to me, his fingers stroke my cheek. "I promise you have much to anticipate."

I feel the blood leaving my face. He watches me steadily and I lick my lips. "Why do you keep me here like this?" I can barely hear my own voice it is so small.

He looks surprised but smiles. "Because I want to. And you'll want it too shortly." He sips his wine and urges me with his free hand to do the same. I do. "I think I was born in the wrong era. Women in Victorian times knew their place. A woman is meant to be submissive to man."

He sips his wine again. I follow his lead, my eyes glued in disbelief to his. "Women had it all then and didn't realize it. They were kept, cared for, taught and protected. But they never appreciated it." He looks over the rim of his glass at me. "But you will Miss Julia." I'm beginning to wonder is he isn't a little mad.

"Just think. A man owned the woman outright. Everything of hers became his. He had total control. He could beat her if she disobeyed or lock her in and none would dare interfere. Not even her own family." He smiles at me but it is a chilling smile and I watch him frozen motionless.

"She came to him unsullied. Pure and innocent and he could mold her any way he chose." His eyes are bright. "He could be a careful, devoted lover and teach her to respond to languid caresses or he could demand a more heady experience and teach her the pleasures of pain and ecstasy." He hands me my glass. "I will teach you both."

I watch him continue to eat and can't tear my eyes from him. "You think of me as your slave?"

He raises his eyes and quirks his brows. An amused smile crosses his lips. "No dear. You are my pet. And you will learn to be an obedient one. Finish your meal and wine." I do. For the second night not tasting the food.

We enter the living room after he clears the dishes. I stand uncertainly as he fusses at the bar getting himself a drink. He returns with drink in one hand and a cigar in the other. ''Face down on the couch.''

I stretch out, the leather cool and soft beneath me. He stretches my arms out tight and clips them to the same hook in the arm of the chair. My breathing is quickening as I wonder what he plans. I hear leather sliding out of loops and can't stop the cry of alarm that slips out of my mouth.

My thighs are pinioned with the belt and I begin to breathe easier. He lifts me and sits down, placing me over his knees. I feel the softness of a cushion under my belly lifting my bottom into the air. Soft music from the stereo fills the air as he moves further down the couch taking me with him. My arms are stretched tighter and my body lifts slightly off the leather. My breasts are brushing it, the cool material exciting my nipples. My feet are under the arm, trapped. My behind is raised over his knees.

''Turn your face to the back of the couch. I want you to think about the sensations you will be feeling. I don't want you distracted by anything.'' My belly twists.

I get a whiff of cigar smoke and then hear him take a sip of his drink. The music washes over me. I see nothing but black leather in front of my eyes. I hear the scrape of a jar opening and tense my buttocks. The sting of his slap is instant. ''Don't clench. I'm going to help you get over this reluctance you have to have your backside used.'' I feel a gob of vaseline spread between my cheeks, his thumb working it into me. Another smack and I tighten again in response. "If you fight me Miss Julia, I will find bigger and bigger things to stretch you with."

I try hard not to but I instinctively fight the intrusion of his cigar tube as it slips in. I hear him click his tongue. I sense him shaking his head as he works the metal tube in and out of my anus. He does this with a steady movement, going very deep and wringing protests from me whenever I clench against it.

I stare at black leather. I feel the steady movement deep inside me. I hear soft music. I hear the occasional sip he takes of his drink. I remain still. I cry when I hear the muted tones and hear him tell Sam to come up. I feel the waves of humiliation wash over me as I hear the elevator doors opening into the living room. He places his left arm around my waist and pulls me even further. My arms strain and I groan. He works the tube deep into me and then leaves it there as he talks to Sam. I have never felt so degraded in my life.

Sam takes his leave and I flinch under the sharp slap on my thighs. The tube is removed. I wait. I hate the waiting the worst. I hear the clink of ice, smell the rich aroma of the cigar. He shifts his position and my arms ease slightly. My legs are picked up and then he is behind me. I feel the hard knob of his penis and brace myself. A stinging blow. I make myself relax, my shrill cry of submission muted in the soft leather. He buggers me mercilessly, stopping and waiting when he nears completion only to start up once more. It goes on forever and I force myself to stay still. Will it never end? He pauses again and I instinctively tense up. I feel the strap released from my thighs and then the sharp kiss of the leather on my back as he lunges deeply and finally finishes. He leans down over my back. ''You only make it harder for yourself Miss Julia.''

He leaves me there and goes to shower, returning maybe an hour later. I have done nothing but cry while he is gone. I hear his sigh but refuse to look at him.

''Stop your nonsense,'' he orders as he releases me. I try but can't stop blubbering. I'm taken into the bathroom and he strips me, pushing me into the shower. I scream as the cold water hits me from all sides and I stop crying. The water warms gradually and he joins me, massaging, rubbing, soaping until I start to cry again but this time with thrills of pleasure.

I have been here a week. Everyday I am kept on the precipice of want, of need. He arouses me before leaving for work and I spend the time tied, wishing he'd return. Lunch time comes and so do I if I have shown improvement in my oral administrations. I've learned to try hard and I am improving.

I spend the afternoon the same way as the morning and am so bored by the time he returns at night that I try hard to do as he wishes so he'll speak to me and make me laugh. I have come to depend on him for everything. I make no decisions. He spends the nights teaching me how to eat different foods, beating me, washing me, making me come and come till I am almost senseless. I can sense that my perspective is shifting and it frightens me that I am beginning to accept this.

I am wearing a lavender corset with matching garters. The stockings are pale. My hair is in its usual pompadour. We have finished dinner and I am attached to a chrome pillar that is about twenty feet in front of the elevator doors. I wait, knowing I am going to hear the muted tones of someone calling for the elevator to be sent down for them. I hope it will be Sam. I am used to him seeing me exposed.

It's not.

It's the man from the employment agency. I'm stunned. I see his eyes widen in pleasure at the sight of me. He stops and openly ogles me. I can't take my eyes from him though I feel my cheeks flame and my whole body start to shake as the meaning of why he must be here finally dawns on me.

"I see it's working out as you wished," he says, reluctantly turning and holding out his hand to shake Mister Caldwell's.

"Yes. She's perfect."

"It took long enough." His eyes swivel back and roam from my head to my feet, lingering on my naked breasts and pubis. I see him lick his lips quickly. "I think it's been almost a year."

"Good things are worth waiting for." Mister Caldwell smiles at me but I'm numb. He takes an envelope from his pocket and hands it to the man. "Five thousand dollars as agreed."

The greedy smile on the man's face makes me wince. I'd been sold. His eyes flick back to me but I can't look at him. I hear the elevator doors open and then Mister Caldwell is directly in front of me. He lifts my chin and my eyes reluctantly raise to his. I feel hurt and can't hide it.

"Tell me."

"You bought me," I whisper.

"No. I paid someone to find you for me." I can't respond to his smile. I'm numb.

"It wasn't me you wanted." I can't explain why this hurts me. I want to believe that it was me he wanted. I didn't want to acknowledge that any young, single, nearly relativeless girl would have done if she'd responded to him as I had. I feel strangely empty. Hollow.

"But it's you I have." He's watching me intently. As if I'm an experiment that needs observation. Maybe that's what I am.

He releases me and I follow him automatically. I can't seem to feel anything. He yanks me out of my clothes and pushes me face down on the bed. I know he's angry at my lassitude but I can't seem to respond. I hardly grunt when he pushes into me. He gives a yell of rage and then grabbing my hairbrush from the night table he beats me horribly, the pain finally penetrates and I begin to fight. My ass is on fire. I can hardly breathe as he presses me into the softness of the bed. At long last I hear his muffled grunt and he collapses on me.

I weep in self-pity and pain. I finally understand why he had me witness the transaction. He'd told me I was his pet and he'd meant it. Just like purchasing a dog, one is as good as another when you view them as all the same.

I no longer feel special. I always thought it was wanting me that made him do the things he did. I always told myself he wanted me so badly he'd go to these lengths to keep me with him. Don't all women at some time in their lives fantasize about some man desiring them so passionately they'd do anything to get them? My fantasy has dissolved. Reality has taken its place.

I am dressed in something different tonight. It is an extremely thin old fashioned shiftlike garment. Very demure. Very feminine. The bodice has buttons to the waist. My nipples show through as faint shadows on white. The bottom ends just above my knees and has a small ruffle. The waist is slightly elasticized so it hugs my body. My hair is in its usual pompadour. My legs and feet are bare. The top three tiny buttons are undone so the garment folds down at the throat and rests on the tops of my breasts. Just a hint of cleavage appears in the gap.

I am seated on a stool about ten feet from the foot of the table. My bracelets are held together with a thin gold chain. I sit quietly watching Mister Caldwell converse with the Frenchman and his son. The son's eyes flick to me often and his father and host mock his impatience gently. This is my third week.

Mister Caldwell looks up. "Come to me Miss Julia," he commands softly, his hand raised.

The Frenchman turns my way and watches my slow approach as he speaks to Mister Caldwell. "Has she made her debut yet?"

"No. This is her first private one. Maybe in a month she will be ready for a public debut."

The Frenchman turns and bows slightly from the waist. "I am honored." My master smiles and takes my hand as I gain his side.

His fingers rub my palm gently and he pulls me

slightly so I face the two men more. I stand between the Frenchman and my master. The son is on my master's other side. Eyes bore into my body everywhere.

"She is charming," the Frenchman murmurs, his hand raising and closing on my breast. I instinctively step back but my master's hand stays me. "Stay still Miss Julia," he murmurs. I feel the old fingers cupping, molding my breasts. My face flames and I can not meet anyone's eye. I can hear the son's breathing becoming faster.

"Absolutely charming. But then I thought so from the first time I met her," he says with a chuckle. I can see myself back in the parking lot. His hands leave me and my master tugs gently on the chain. I fall to my knees.

I feel his fingers stroking my neck and my skin tingles. Deft fingers work their way through my hair, massaging, kneading. I can feel myself shifting. Fearful anticipation is melting into yearning. My mouth goes slack.

"She loves to be stroked," Mister Caldwell whispers, his fingers continuing their magic. He pulls me closer to him. My chin rests on his thigh. His fingers urge me further and I feel his thumb brush my lips. "Suck," he orders and I do but it is his penis he slips into my mouth.

Fingers of steel hold me still as I struggle against doing this intimate thing in front of others. My arms are pinned against the side of the chair, the penis is deep in my throat and his hand holds me still. I start to gag and he eases the pressure imperceptively. "Suck," he murmurs but I cannot. I can feel the tears. I can feel the lump forming in my throat. I feel fingers, light gentle fingers between my legs. I whimper as they soothe and caress. I am unable to hold out long against the insidious, sensuous manipulations and I begin to suck in time with the finger's movements.

Someone is breathing hard but I can not tell if it is I or one of the men. I am going over the edge. The pressure builds and I am working myself on the fingers as hard as I can. I feel the spurt, hear the grunt and then the fingers are gone and I am writhing on air. I swallow and swallow, my pleas muffled and ignored as the prick slowly shrinks in my mouth. Fingers lessen the pressure on my head and it falls from my mouth. I am panting, my hips still rocking, the need still strong.

His hands soothe my cheek. I open my eyes and all is as before. The men seated and talking as they drink their brandy. Only the bright light in the son's eyes tell me it is not over.

I stay kneeling at his side, my head on his knee. His fingers stroke and caress my forehead, cheek and lips. I am boiling with need. My insides are twisted and heavy. My clit is engorged and I try to work my heel under me but a quick flick of his finger on my cheek stops any attempts. His fingers reach down and I feel the buttons being loosened as he continues his conversation without faltering. Fingers stroke my nipples and I can't suck in enough air. My legs clench as the intensity builds. I hear myself whimpering deep in my throat and then he's pushing back his chair and standing.

I'm on the floor in a daze. My hands reach for my loins but he picks up the chain and pulls me upright. "Don't be naughty Miss Julia," he chides me gently and then hands the chain to the Frenchman. I'm stunned. I never thought about him giving me to anyone else. I can't quite take it in and I watch in disbelief as he walks away.

"Don't look so tragic cherie," the Frenchman says, tilting my chin so I must look up at him. "You will not be sorry."

I feel a lead weight in the pit of my stomach. Nothing is as it should be. His son comes behind me and grabs my breasts, his fingers hard and cruel. I start, the pain releasing me from immobility. I yank my hands down hard and the chain is ripped from the old fingers as I duck under his son's arms and run for the door Mister Caldwell disappeared through. It's locked and I bang on the door, screaming for him, frantic. I hear laughter and a sigh.

"Go get her Pierre. I think it will be livelier than I anticipated."

I feel myself swung up onto a shoulder, tears running down my cheeks as I cry for my master. I refuse to believe this is happening until I am thrown onto a bed in another bedroom. Pierre is on me and ripping my shift before I can take a breath. I smell the brandy and then feel his mouth on my breast. I'm panting and screaming and trying to kick him and he utters what I can only assume is a curse and bites down on my tender flesh. My angry scream shifts to a screech of pain in midstream.

His weight leaves me abruptly and I open tear filled eyes to see his father holding him back by the collar. I can hardly gulp air my heart is pounding so hard. My fingers seek out the torn flesh and I look at the blood on my hand in horror. I try to rise but the older man turns my way and utters a harsh, "Stay!" and I do, cowed by his sudden commanding appearance. I lay still listening to him berate his son in French. I watch the color fade and darken in the young man's face. I see the flash of anger, the resentment and finally the acceptance of what his father is saying to him. I feel like I'm at the movies. As if this isn't really happening in front of me.

The father releases the man's collar and smiles, his hand on his shoulder. "Go into the bathroom and relieve yourself in the sink. Then when you are calm I will show you the right way to make love to a woman.''

I watch the young man do his father's bidding, though a little self-consciously. My eyes turn and he sits on the edge of the bed, shaking his head sadly. ''You will forgive Pierre. He is not as experienced as he thinks and has trouble controlling himself.'' He takes my hands and clips the chain to a hook in the headboard. I lay shaking before him. His smile is slow and sweet. ''I do not want the little love bird to fly while I go get something to wipe her cut with.''

I watch him, his tender smile lingering in my thoughts as he disappears into the bathroom. Surely this man will not hurt me. He steps through the door with a damp cloth in his hand and gently wipes my breast and then my hand. I give him a smile and feel it trembling on my lips. His hand strokes my cheek softly. ''Between us we will make a good lover of my Pierre. Yes?'' he asks in a whisper just as Pierre appears in the room.

He sees the cloth in his father's hand and awkwardly apologizes to the man. ''You do a disservice to your host when you ruin his possessions.''

''Papa she is nothing but a whore,'' the man exclaims in exasperation and I feel myself wince at the word. I'm instantly back in the church, the priest lecturing me about the downfall that would await me if I chose such a path.

''She is not a whore. She is your host's possession. A cherished possession he is kind enough to share with us.''

I see the disbelief in the younger man's eyes. See his rage building. ''You may call it what you will but it makes her no less.''

I watch the old hands clench. I see the adam's apple move as he swallows deeply. I am oddly touched that he wishes to protect me. I wish my hands were free to pat his in understanding. "You do your mama a dishonor if you believe that."

Eyes widen in shock. "What do you say?"

"You dishonor your mama if you believe this women is a whore." His words are so low, so steady that I find myself straining not to miss a one.

"You are not saying. . . ."

"Yes Pierre. Your mama was sold to me by a poor family. I had seen her in a village and made them an offer they couldn't refuse." He sighs with memory. The silence is total. "I thought I would amuse myself with her. Much to my regret I even shared her with a few people I owed favors to." He shakes his head sadly. "It was done more often in those days than now." His finger slowly traces the line of my jaw. "I taught her all I wished her to know. All she did not wish to learn. I was a hard taskmaster with her. But I came to realize that I truly cared for her and when my seed grew in her belly I married her." I can feel the slight shaking his fingers have as they move slowly to and fro across my jaw. "I never regretted my decision and cherished her for the rest of her life."

"Papa." I watch the shocked disbelief in the younger voice reach through his father's reverie. He removes his hand from me. Strangely I already miss the soft caress.

"Yes Pierre I know you cannot grasp it but as I say, things were done differently then." I watch him lift his head, the command back in his voice. "But you will heed my words about this little bird. She is a gift from your host. Something to be taken care of, to take delight in, but always to be returned in the same condition as you received her. Not damaged. No seed growing in her belly."

His eyes turn back to me and I find myself smiling at

him. His gentle words soothe me and make me happy. I feel better about myself than I have since the employment agency man was here. He is rubbing my hip with the heel of his hand. I like it.

He leans down and kisses me gently, his hand moving up my side, tickling my ribs, brushing my nipple, stroking the length of my bare arm. My breath catches in my throat. Things start to shift in my mind. My hands are released and he pulls me to my feet. My head swims and I lean into him lightly. He holds me and strokes my back, my neck, my hair that is in total disarray, strands hanging down my back. He takes my shoulders and pushes me away slightly, bringing my hands to his lips. He sucks on each finger in turn and kisses them. My breath is uneven. I feel my arms lifted, my feet leave the floor for a second and then I am poised, almost on tiptoe, from a hook in the ceiling.

I turn worried eyes to him but he smiles that sweet smile and my fear melts. He rubs my neck, lightly, ever so lightly. Shivers run through me. He kisses my lips, my eyes, my cheek, my ear. I am melting. I feel his tongue on my collarbone and arch upwards. I want to feel his tongue on my breast but he teases me and returns to my neck. Delicious tremors race up my spine.

He leaves me and I watch with anxious eyes for his return. He leaves my field of sight and I start to turn but a sharp smack on my bottom stops me. "Stay as you are," he whispers directly behind me. A soft cloth covers my eyes and I am in darkness.

"Why Papa?"

"It heightens their awareness. She can not know because she can not see so it all becomes delicious fearful anticipation. Fear can be a powerful aphrodisiac if it is used the right way." I feel knuckles lightly running up and down the length of my arms. Gooseflesh rises behind it. "See how her breathing has quickened. Watch her breasts rise and fall. See the pulse beating crazily in her neck." The rapid pulse is kissed and it becomes even faster. "Her awareness of her body is enhanced. Each touch will feel more intense."

I feel a whisper of air just above my breast. Someone's breath. My nipples harden. Hands stroke my chest. Lips lick along my shoulders. Is it one or both of them? I feel buttons opening, fingers stroking my ribs. I ache for them to reach my breast. The thin fabric is brushed aside and the cool air caresses my breasts. I am panting. My thighs tighten as the familiar feeling starts to build.

My back is stroked. My neck. My shoulder. My chest. I wait. I can hardly suck in air. My heart is pounding. Why don't they touch my breasts? A jolt like lightening hits me as the two warm mouths simultaneously latch onto each breast. It is incredible and I almost orgasm from the intensity. They lick and suck and then lick some more. I strain at my bonds. I want desperately to hold each head in place so it can't leave. "Don't stop," I whisper in desperation, my vaginal walls pulsing as I try to find a way to finish. I give a wail of disappointment when both leave at the same time.

Silence.

I clench my thighs together and writhe in frustration. Tears trickle out of my eyes. "Please." My voice is a harsh agonized whisper.

Silence.

I'm frantic that they left and I didn't hear them. I strain my ears. I try to hold my breath to listen better. Silence. I'll go mad.

Hands soothe my back and I try to turn. I want them on my breasts. I'm held in place. They cup my breasts from behind and slowly pull on the nipples. Flashes of intense need shoot straight to my loins. My breath is ragged. I'm barely able to get enough air and then I feel a tongue suck in my clitoris and with one flick of his tongue I'm gushing, screaming in ecstasy as wave after wave of sensation wash over me.

I sag, oblivious of the pain in my wrists. I'm held, supported and taken off the hook. I lean heavily against whoever holds me. Gentle hands lower me onto the bed. I hear heavy breathing.

"Go on son. There is no need to wait longer. We have all night. Put on a condom before you start."

I feel my shift pushed up and dazedly open my legs. I am wet from someone's mouth and he slips in easily. I can hear his heavy breathing, feel the swipe of a tongue on my breast. I feel the tension in his arms as he holds me. He's done soon after.

My breathing has slowed and Pierre has risen. I lay quietly, my arms reattached to the wall. The sound of running water reaches me. I wonder when the older man will want me? How will he want me? I feel myself dozing.

I wake to the touch of fingers teasing my nipples. I can not tell whose fingers they are. All night I cannot tell whose fingers they are. I'm caressed and licked on every part of my body and I lick and suck when instructed to. They keep me high on sensation, only allowing me to orgasm infrequently but even then it seems more of a relief than an experience. I'm washed in the shower, turned and entered. I'm bent and used as I don't like and I hear the gentle laugh of the older man. "Women like this the least. They don't like to make this submission to men. They know they are supposed to think it is dirty and then when they are aroused by it they feel guilty." He is gentle in his movements and not especially big so I do not clench against him. "You are a charming pet little one," he murmurs and then finishes.

The night goes on and on, his son is young and has a prodigious amount of stamina and recuperative power.

When he becomes a little too eager and harsh, I hear the older one's gentle voice bidding him to ease up. I am awash in sensation. I do not even think about when one is with me the other is watching.

My arms are lifted and I am attached to the hook on the ceiling. I am limp, my body exhausted. I feel an arm encircle my waist and know what is about to happen. The first sharp sting hits me unexpectedly hard. I gasp and choke as my breath rushes from my body. The blows that follow are heavy, fast and my behind is liquid fire. I think they take turns. I scream and scream and finally they stop. I'm twisting and turning, my legs clenching and tensing against the pain. My ankles are lifted and my arms scream in protest. I feel them bound behind one of the men. His penis slips into me. Another body behind me and then I'm sandwiched between them and screaming again as he enters me from behind. The pain takes over everything and I continue to scream as they take their pleasure together. I pass out before they finish. I wake up hooked to my own bed.

I feel betrayed. The sweet old man had hurt me. Had helped his son to hurt me. And Mister Caldwell had let them. Chills run down my spine.

Mister Caldwell enters my room. Silently as always. He stands at the door and watches me for a long time. I'm very uneasy under his contemplative stare. A sudden thought terrorizes me. Suppose he gives me away for good. I feel the blood leave my face. I see his head tilt slightly as he studies me.

"Tell me." The command is so quiet. So serious.

I watch him approach me and search his eyes. They

are steady and dark. Unreadable. I lick my lips and swallow. "Would you give me to someone for keeps?" I can barely hear my own words.

I watch his eyebrows shoot up. It's as though the thought had never occurred to him before. I find myself flushing under his gaze and my eyes drop. My chin is cupped and lifted. "Why would I do that?"

I shake my head, suddenly at a loss for words. His thumb is moving along my jaw and I lean into the light pressure. He smiles. "Why would I give you to anyone else? You give me pleasure."

I shrug, feeling foolish. I want him to understand how I feel but can't form the words to explain. I struggle to express my fears. "And when I don't any longer?"

He lightly kisses my lips. "But you do and always will because you obey me whether you wish to or not."

"Last night. . . ."

"I paid off a debt. Nothing more." The topic is to be dropped. He unclips me and I remain silent. He strokes my cheek and gives me another smile. "I have a surprise for you tonight."

"For me?"

"Yes for you," he says with an indulgent chuckle. He removes his robe and motions towards the bathroom. We shower together, my hands free for the first time, his hands loving and soft. It is the first time I have soaped his body. I like the feel of him. He makes no move to have me but holds me close and I think I hear a sigh above the sound of the water. I feel his hands on my striped rear end. They are gentle and soothing and I lean into his hard body happily. The warm steam cocoons us. The water washes over us unnoticed for a long time.

I am given the freedom of my room for the day. I wander around feeling decidedly odd. I have no idea what to do. I'm not used to so much freedom. I turn on the television but have no interest in the programs and turn it off. I sift through the titles of the movies in the cabinet. Some of them frighten me and I quickly close the door. I stare at the door of the other cabinet for a long time and finally morbid curiosity compels me to open it. My eyes travel in fascinated horror from one thing to the next.

It contains whips of every description. Bamboo canes, riding crops, paddles. There are gags in different sizes and shapes, one particularly vicious looking with small sharp spikes coming out of what looks like a bit for a horse. I feel tingles of dread travel my spine and I shudder. There are dildos in all sizes from the norm to the deadly. One is two pronged and ridged with small hard rubber spokes. I realize it's to impale both places at one time and remembering how much pain the two smooth penis's had caused me I feel my stomach revolt and turn. I can't keep looking at the rest and slam the doors shut, panting with fear. Why does he have these things?

I rub my arms and walk away. I can't look out the window because it is too high. I wouldn't dare try to open any doors but the bathroom after my last experience. So I sit on the bed and wait. The waiting is always the hardest.

Waiting to be unhooked. Waiting for the first smack. Waiting to see what he will do. Waiting for him to come to me. Waiting for him to make me come when I feel I'll surely go mad if I don't.

I wander into the bathroom and study my body in the mirrors. My skin seems slacker than before. I don't do anything and it's starting to show. I gently rub a finger over the bruise on my breast. You can just about see the teeth marks. That had hurt more than the worst time I'd been caned. The pain in my rear always seemed to eventually merge and sear into my cunt enabling me to have mind boggling intense orgasms.

My eyes lift and meet themselves in the mirror. No that's not true. It's only Mister Caldwell's beatings that do that. I see my brows lift in wonder at the same time I feel them. I had only felt pain when the Frenchmen had spanked me. It had never been anything but pain. It hadn't rushed down to my cunt to meet the invading penis as it did with Mister Caldwell.

I sink down to the thick carpeting. I'm dumbfounded. I came with the Frenchmen but it was a necessary thing my body required. It wasn't the mind shattering experience I feel with Mister Caldwell. Is that love? I see my hand starting to stroke myself and come out of my thoughts quickly, snatching my hand away. Panic races through my brain and I quickly jump up and wash my hands. Over and over. Suppose he guesses? I smell my hand and wash again. I rub scented cream into them and then wash again and cream again. I'm not allowed to do that. My thoughts flash to the double dildo in the closet and I wash a few more times.

"Have you been naughty Miss Julia?"

His low voice makes me jerk guiltily and I turn eyes wide with fear towards him. He's coming closer to me and I put my right hand behind me. I see his brows raise questioningly and then the dismay enter his eyes. I hear his sigh as he lifts his hand.

My heart is pounding. My mouth is dry. I start to cry as I put my hand in his. He raises it to his nose and sniffs. His eyes bore into mine knowingly. I see his lips thin and harden and I cry harder, my stammering explanation unintelligible.

I feel so guilty that I disappointed him as he turns and leaves but the guilt is quickly wiped out by the fear that invades my body when I see him returning with the hooded mask. "No." It squeaks out like a strangled whisper and I panic at the grim expression on his face. I try to run but his fingers form a vise around my wrist and I'm spun around and my hands clipped together. The hood descends and I feel it tighten. I'm totally disoriented when he tosses me on his shoulder and takes me to another room.

I'm sucking in breath by the time he puts me on the floor. My hands are unclipped and I stand still. I can not hear him over my tortured breathing and I'm afraid. I hate the not knowing. I hate feeling as if I could be standing on the edge of a cliff, one wrong move meaning my downfall. I try to control my breathing. My heart could be a speeding locomotive.

Leather touches my chest. My arms are raised and I feel some kind of halter encircling my breasts, neck and under my arms. I hear the click of clips and I'm pulled forward and bent over what feels like a table. My arms are drawn up behind me and clipped tightly to the leather. I feel his hand on my neck to hold me down and I tighten every muscle in my body. He makes me wait.

I don't even hear the hiss before it strikes, the sudden pain jerking me forward sharply. It bites into my flesh and I flail my legs uselessly against the pain. Five, six, seven times and then I'm jerked upright and on my feet. I'm pulled slightly upwards and know I'm attached to a hook in the ceiling. My legs are doing a strange sort of dance as they try to find a position to alleviate the pain. One arm is let loose and the fingers shoved in my mouth. It's pulled out and he pushes it against my mound.

"Make yourself come."

I freeze. I'm not allowed to do this. I can't do this knowing he's watching me. I don't move. His voice is directly behind me. "You wanted to do it pet. So do it now."

I don't move. He hits the top of my thighs and I scream in pain. "Do it." I'm writhing in agony and he lashes my tender thighs again. My hand creeps lower quickly and I move my fingers.

"Open your legs." I do. I'm still fighting and tensing against the pain that seems to vibrate and hum along my legs. What did he use? Something wickedly thin and cutting. My fingers move but I can't feel anything but the pain.

Tears are pouring out of my eyes and I feel them leaking out of the leather. I can't stop crying and he slashes me again. My fingers move harder and after a long time I finally start to feel some response. It grows slowly and my breath is starting to quicken with the feelings. I don't know where he is and it makes me nervous but soon I care for nothing more than to reach my climax. I bite my lower lip and work my fingers harder and then I'm there. It's a relief mixed with embarrassment and pain.

"You've been a bad girl." His whisper hardly penetrates and then his arm is around my waist and he's pounding my backside with a paddle. I'm confused and hurting and then he stops and my hand is pushed back again.

He makes me do it to myself four times, beating me between each and then I'm let down and tied face down on the table. I feel a dildo pushed into me, another into my ass and then I hear faint clicks. They're vibrators and the humming grows and grows as it titillates and hurts at the same time. I'm groaning by the time I come but he doesn't stop them.

"Remember the feeling," he whispers in my ear as I feel the now painful build up again once more. Five times with no respite. I'm almost crazy with the intensity of each but each is more painful than the last. I can't breathe I'm sobbing so hard. My pleading for mercy stopped long ago. I have to concentrate just on enduring.

I spend the afternoon hooked to the bed. I would give anything for a cool wet cloth to ease the tender bud. My lower body throbs and pulsates still. I wonder if I'll ever be able to come again.

He makes me eat with him in the dining room. My rear is so sore I can barely sit still through the meal. He watches me intently all the while but I concentrate on trying to eat and not choke.

"Needless to say there'll be no surprise tonight."

I nod but don't answer. "Finish your wine and come to me Miss Julia."

I do. I know my forlorn expression doesn't sway him but I can't seem to have any other. He pushes my shoulder and I kneel, obediently taking his shaft in my mouth. I hear his sigh as he lays his head back, his hand negligently tugging on my hair now and then. I feel his thighs tense beneath me and hear the distant grunt. I swallow now without thought. I clean him and wait, my cheek on his thigh. I smell his cigar, get a whiff of brandy as he exhales deeply. His fingers absently stroke the hair back from my cheek and I begin to relax.

I spend the evening just like that. He is quiet, content to remain at the table and sip his brandy for a long time. He smokes three cigars before he brings me back to my room. I wasn't sure if I wanted to know what he thought of.

I'm lying in bed waiting to be let up. I look toward the high windows and see a cloud glide gently by. A small smile lifts my lips. I like clouds. Always have. I like the wispy ones that seem to stretch out forever and never get thinner. I like the thick heavy ones that remind me of scoops of vanilla ice cream. I even like the dark forbidding ones that promise mayhem and storm.

I haven't been outside in five weeks. I haven't felt the sun on my face or breathed in anything but air conditioned air. The sadness engulfs me as I suddenly realize how much I miss it.

Mister Caldwell is watching me from the doorway when I turn from the window. I flush knowing he's seen my pensive look. I still get the feeling sometimes he can read my mind.

"Would you like your surprise tonight?" he asks quietly as he unclips me. I can't stop the sudden smile that spreads across my face as I nod eagerly. His finger strokes my cheek and I turn quickly and kiss it before he can move. I surprise myself with the unexpected gesture but he seems pleased and smiles at me gently.

We shower after he attaches me to the wall and meticulously shaves my underarms and pubis. He teases me as he soaps me, leaving me panting for more. He takes his time washing himself, ignoring me as if I wasn't there. I'm ready to beg but then his mouth is where I want it and I breathe in steam and float on the sensations he causes. He stands up and works over my chest with his tongue and then he's inside me and I'm there at the same time as he is. A first for us. He kisses the tip of my nose and leads me out of the steamy stall.

I pace my room all day. I'm dying of curiosity about the surprise. Will it be clothes? Real clothes? My entire wardrobe consists of a few Victorian shifts and corsets in different colors. I haven't had a pair of panties or bra on in five weeks.

I hug myself excitedly. The last surprise was dinner and the theatre. Will he take me? Will I be going outside? I feel like my heart is turning over with excitement. Will he never get home from work?

I pace. I have no watch or clock so I don't know the

time. I look up at the windows but it is cloudy and I don't know where the sun would be in the sky. I pace some more and turning see him standing in the doorway. I stop and stare, my heart beating fast. I have never gotten used to the silent door and thick rugs. It always throws me out of balance to see him suddenly there. I can't keep the excitement from my voice.

"Hi," I say and I can hear the breathless higher pitch. That wonderful smile covers his lips and I relax. I'm surprised at how tight I had been.

Mister Caldwell moves into the room but doesn't shut the door. I look at him questioningly, noticing no packages, nothing on him. The doorway darkens and I turn surprised eyes towards it. I feel myself sway as my belly twists. It is filled with the largest human being I have ever seen.

He walks, no lumbers is a better word, into the room and stands beside Mister Caldwell who immediately looks like a child beside the giant. The man stands six foot six or seven and is barrel chested. His legs are massive like tree limbs and I can't tear my eyes from his hands. They look as if they could pick my up and literally pull me into two pieces. I start to shake.

"This is Lars." I see his head nod and notice his eyes are dim. "Lars this is Miss Julia." He nods again and looks around without interest. I can't stop shaking. I can't meet Mister Caldwell's eyes. I'm terrified of what I might see. Please no, I scream to myself.

A hand cups my chin and lifts it. I'm trapped by his quizzical gaze. I'm too frightened to even notice the smile. "Tell me."

I open my mouth but my jaw trembles and I have to snap it shut. I swallow hard and try again. All I manage is a plaintive, "Please."

"Please what?" His eyes are so steady.

"He'll kill me," I blurt out and then start to cry.

I'm pulled close and held. "He's not here to kill you. He's the surprise."

"I don't understand," I wail, my terror receding slowly as I feel the gentle circular motions on my back. I love being held like this. Stroked. Cared for.

"Lars will stay with you and this way you can have the run of the entire apartment." I pull back and look at him.

"You mean when you're at work?" I sniff.

He nods his head and brushes a tear from my cheek. "Exactly."

"Unchained?" I asked hesitantly.

"If you're good."

I give him a tentative smile. There are places in the apartment I haven't seen and am curious about. "I'm sorry," I murmur, knowing he doesn't like tears.

He gives me a lopsided smile and then becomes serious. "Lars is intensely loyal to me. Don't ever make the mistake of trying to pit one against the other." I'm bobbing my head in agreement, not able to think that far yet. The thought of not being kept in one room all day is a heady experience after so long.

"Come with me."

He takes my arms and leads me into the bathroom where Lars is undressing. I pull back slightly and feel the pressure of his fingers increase. I start shaking all over again as I stare at the figure in front of me. His shirt lifts over his shoulders and it appears as if large rocks are rolling around under his skin as his muscles bunch and flex. His belt is at least two inches thick and I almost sag when I hear it whipped out of the loops. His pants drop and I'm staring at two massive cheeks that are hard as rocks. He turns and a mist seems to envelope me. I feel myself sway and then arms tighten on my shoulders. A soft stinging on my cheeks makes the mist evaporate.

"Take her Lars." I can't believe what I'm hearing and stand helplessly in his grasp as I watch him approach. I can't tear my eyes from his penis. It is at least a foot long and not even hard yet. I'm cringing but Mister Caldwell's hands are like steel. I shudder as a massive paw reaches for me. I'm paralyzed. I want to scream, yell, run but all I do is stand frozen.

His hands close around my waist and lift me effortlessly. I support myself on his arms and I might be touching concrete. I brace to be squeezed into nothingness but I hardly feel his fingers around me. I look down and see them spanning my waist like a massive belt. He's carrying me to the tub that is half full. I'm held out in front of him like you carry a wet baby. He places me in the foot of the tub and I stand there confused.

"Kneel down Miss Julia." I turn startled eyes sideways and Mister Caldwell is beside me. I kneel. Lars lowers himself and the tub water rises a good four inches. He fills the tub, something I thought no one could do. His massive legs are on either side of me and I feel as if I am in a steel trap.

"Take his penis in your hands and bring him off."

My eyes once more look at the huge tool and I shudder violently. It has grown slightly and is even larger. "Do as you're told Miss Julia or he'll use it in other places." His voice is so casual, as if he were telling me to get him a drink of water. I reach out and touch the shaft tentatively. It moves under my fingers as I start to manipulate it. My fingers work automatically, my eyes glued in shocked horror as it continues to grow.

"I want you to remember the size of his penis Miss Julia. Lars is slow to arouse and you'll be safe with him. I repeat he is intensely loyal to me. If you ever try to use him or the freedom of the apartment to do something I wouldn't like I will have him put it up your ass."

My hands stop for just a second and then continue. My master's voice is so soft, so menacing in its very lack of emotion. "Think of the damage. You'd be irreparably harmed for life. Maybe killed. Think of the pain."

I nod automatically. I can barely span the circumference with my two hands. I never thought I had small hands till this moment. I watch in fascinated horror as it continues to grow and redden. I would have accused anyone who told me of such proportions of exaggerating grossly.

"Faster Miss Julia," Mister Caldwell urges and I obey. I can see the man's thighs tensing. The muscles bunch and stick out like knobs. I hear him suck in a deep breath and then he shoots, the gism hitting me square in the chest. I keep up my movements and stare at the huge gobs of white hitting me and then trickling down inside my shift. I feel him relax and then he sits up straighter and my hands are suddenly empty.

Lars smiles a lazy smile and stands up. "Thank you Miss Julia," he says as he lifts me from the tub. It sounds as if I had lent him a cup of sugar or something. I stand where he puts me and watch without moving as he slowly redresses. He nods once more at me and lumbers out the door. I stupidly look down at my hands and can't think what to do. I stand there.

Fingers at my buttons and I look up and see Mister Caldwell. He's naked and his once magnificent body looks insignificant by comparison. I lift my arms and the shift is removed. I shiver in the air conditioned air. He attaches the bracelets low in the shower and pulls me back so I bend. I feel soap being lathered into my crack and then the hard knob of his shaft. I force myself to relax. He takes his time, leaning over me soaping my breasts till my mouth falls open and I become a mass of sensuality. His hands roam lower and lower and I wait impatiently for him to continue further. He's easing in and out of me with a slow steady pace and I feel the ball of fire starting to converge and burn. He leans over me, blocking the steady fall of water on my back. He pushes deeper and I bite my lips. His lips lick my ear. I turn so he can put it into my ear but instead he whispers, "Just think of the difference. Think of the consequences. Think what it would feel like plowing into your rear." I shiver and then his hands move lower and the forces converge with lightening speed and I'm pushing back hard against him, wanting him deeper and deeper as my body pulsates and throbs.

I wake the next morning and wait impatiently for him. My heart flutters with excitement. The door opening catches my eye and I lay absolutely still when I see Lars walk in. He approaches the bed in his slow lumbering way and smiles his lazy smile. "Good morning Miss Julia," he says as he leans over me and unclips me. I watch but his eyes never seem to notice my nudity. I'm terribly disappointed Mister Caldwell didn't come.

I sit up and look at the open door, waiting for him to enter the room silently like always but he doesn't and I finally get up and go into the bathroom. Lars is adjusting the water temperature. "Hurry up Miss Julia. Breakfast is cooking." He stands there and waits."

"I have to go to the bathroom Lars."

"I'll wait Miss Julia." I feel the blush suffusing my face but he just stands there and looks at me patiently. His eyes are dim and I wonder if he's a little slow. He doesn't move so I finally sit and pee. He never looks in my direction. I approach the shower and am surprised when he follows me in and attaches me to the wall. "Mister Caldwell will be here in a moment."

And then he leaves, his shoulders wet and his hair dripping. He seems to have one speed. Slow and steady.

The steam fills the stall and I wait, breathing in the hot moist air slowly. Drops form on my nose and I shake my head to fling them off. More form immediately. I wait.

I'm stretched tight, my arms high above my head. I like the feeling. Much better than just being attached. When I'm stretched like this I feel things more keenly. My body always feels poised for the next sensation.

I'm aware of the difference in temperatures on my body. My buttocks and shoulders are against the cool wall of the shower that didn't heat up before I stopped the steam from reaching it. The rest of me is bathed in hot moist air. It seems to swirl and caress me. Drops form on my nipples and I see them drip from the peaks. I feel rivulets run down the crease where hip and thigh join. My toes curl with the delicious feeling.

The door opens and I smile. Dark eyes watch me for a moment and then I see his own smile through the mist. "Good morning," he says, hands reaching out to stroke and tease my nipple. I suck in hot moist air before answering.

"Good morning."

He lathers me and shaves me, his fingers staying after the razor leaves. I'm squirming and shifting feet by the time he enters me and then I want nothing more than to feel him in me for all time.

My happiness fades when he attaches the short chain to my bracelets. "You said if I was good," I protest but he just smiles and kisses my lips."

"When you prove you've been good."

He holds a sleeveless shift for me to step into and I do, watching him pull and tie the dainty ribbon that holds it above my breasts. He leans down and places a soft kiss on each nipple, the damp spot showing my nipples more clearly through the thin fabric.

We're served breakfast by Lars. He smiles when Mister Caldwell compliments him on the waffles and bacon and then disappears into the kitchen. I can hear the sound of pots and pans in a sink. I turn confused eyes to the head of the table. "Lars cooked this?"

"He's an excellent cook, bodyguard, housekeeper, mechanic and friend." He takes a sip of hot coffee and chews a mouthful of bacon. "I notice you're putting on weight. Getting soft. Next week I'll arrange for an aerobics instructor to come three times a week."

"I used to jog. I could do that again."

"The apartment is too small." He takes another sip and I gather my courage.

"If Lars went with. . . . ."

"Lars will show you how to use some of the weight machines I use." End of discussion.

He rises, kisses me on the cheek and then leaves. I sit there unsure of what to do. Lars comes in and clears the dishes and suddenly nervous about being alone I follow him into the kitchen. "Do you wish more tea Miss Julia?"

"No thank you." I look around and look at all the appliances. "Can I help you Lars."

He glances at my bracelets and shakes his head. I feel so awkward. I'm dying to explore the apartment and yet I'm afraid to by myself. "I could dust," I offer, knowing it would be a good excuse to go from room to room but again the huge head shakes negatively.

"That's my job Miss Julia."

"Yes I know but. . . ." He turns and looks pointedly at me and I falter and stop. His eyes are dim but steady like Mister Caldwell's. I sit at the table and watch him wash and dry the dishes. "Have you known Mister Caldwell long?"

"Yes." No more. He keeps wiping the pans. I rise and walk out of the kitchen, half expecting to be called back. I'm not. I go into the living room and sit down. I glance through a magazine on the table. I rise. I walk to the bar and read the bottle labels. I look at a door on the far wall but can't bring myself to touch the knob. I meander through the room and end up in front of the elevator. Is it up here? Is it on the ground floor? I turn and see Lars watching me intently.

I feel my heart quicken and hastily try to explain. "I wasn't . . . I mean I . . . I didn't. . . ."

The giant nods his head and continues to wipe his hands on the dishtowel. "I'm glad to hear that Miss Julia. It would make me very sad to have to hurt a little thing like you."

I swallow and nod, the warning clear and unmistakable even though it is said so conversationally. I hurry to my room and stay there for the rest of the afternoon. It is too much freedom after so long. It makes me nervous.

We eat a marvelous dinner of filet mignon, wild rice and a ceasar's salad. I feel all thumbs as I cut my meat. It's something I haven't done in a long time. The knife slips and a piece of meat slides off the plate. I blush and don't look up. No comment is made.

Mister Caldwell pulls back my chair and I stand. He takes my hand as he walks into the living room. I'm awkward again. I am always led by the arm. Now I walk side by side holding his hand. I'm disoriented. He sits on the couch and I stay standing. i'm not used to this much freedom. I don't know what to do.

"Sit down Miss Julia." I do, happy to be told what to do. I sit and stare ahead of me. My hands clasp each other. I feel exposed, vulnerable and I want nothing more than to run to my room. I jump at the sound of his voice.

"Do you like to be read to?"

"I don't know. I haven't been since I was a little girl."

"Then we shall see," he says with a smile and rising goes to a floor to ceiling shelf and takes down a thick volume. "Are you familiar with Edgar Allen Poe?"

"I've seen his movies on television."

He smiles that special smile and my heart flutters. "That is Hollywood. Not Poe." He sits in the corner of the couch and beckons me to him. I go eagerly, once more feeling safe as his arms go around me so he can hold the book in front of him. I snuggle deep into the crook of his body, surrounded and feeling safe wedged between him and the couch. I hear his soft chuckle. I stretch my legs out the length of the couch as his are and I sigh as he begins to read a poem called Annabel Lee. I become lost in the story. His voice is low and deep and I shut my eyes and try to visualize what he reads. He stops and shuts the book. I blink back tears.

"It's so sad," I whisper.

"What is? That she died or that they loved so deeply?"

"Both."

"Have you ever been deeply in love Miss Julia?"

I stare at his hands holding the book and think about the question. "I'm not sure," I finally murmur, praying he won't pursue it because I can't explain it myself. Am I in love with him or am I just dependent on him?

Will I leave him forever if I get the chance? Do I want to?

I don't know.

Mister Caldwell has been quiet, as if reading my thoughts again. I can feel my breath coming faster as I start to panic at the thought. I jump at the sound of his voice above my head. "Do you like being read to?"

I nod my head against his chest. "Very much. You make it seem so real." My voice falters and I take a deep breath. "I like the sound of your voice." I wait for his reaction but all he does is give me a quick hug and then opens the book and searches for another poem.

He reads one then another, his hand stroking my arm as he speaks. His palm grazes along my hipbone and my breath quickens. It lightly traces my belly, my ribs, till settling on my breast. I don't hear the words any longer just the deep voice flowing over me as if it is caressing me gently. I'm pulling in air through my mouth when he finishes the piece he is reading.

He is talking to me and I try to rouse myself so I hear his words but then the two tones sound and I come alert at once. His hand poises on my collarbone as he listens to Lars' voice speak to someone downstairs. Lars walks toward us and informs Mister Caldwell that M. Lafouche is on his way up.

I feel the blood drain from my lips and flinch. His hands tighten on me as I try to rise. "Easy girl. The debt was paid."

I'm stiff and tense. I don't want to see the Frenchman again. I want to be in my bedroom. I hear the whoosh of the doors opening and lay there against Mister Caldwell as the man approaches, his faced wreathed in smiles. I lower my eyes and study the button in front of them.

"Ah what a charming scene. I hope I have not intruded." I hear the sound of fingers being kissed.

"What a delightful state of deshabille you keep the little bird in."

"What is it you want Lafouche?"

"You sound angry my friend. What is it? Surely not that little affair of my son getting overzealous for a moment. It was a small bite nothing more," the man dismisses lightly. I want to see Mister Caldwell's face but can't. I feel his body tense under mine. His hand covers my breast lightly. I still don't look at the man who used me so badly with his son.

"Your business Lafouche?"

I hear the slight hesitation in his voice. "I thought perhaps. . . ."

"You thought wrong." Arms tighten around me. I have to brace myself against the force. I'm sure he appears relaxed to any other.

I can see the Frenchman's legs in front of me but I lift my eyes no higher. Mister Caldwell's heart thuds beneath my ear. His hands lifts from my breast and traces the line of my jaw. His thumb brushes my lips and they open of their own will but his fingers are back down to my breast where they lay lightly on the hardening nipple.

I hear sounds vibrating against my cheek and realize their voices have risen. I haven't been listening. The fingers are so distracting with their lazy, slow, sensuous movements.

"But my client. . . . ."

"Is your affair."

"Only for one night. I give you my word she won't be harmed."

"Lars will show you out."

"Mon Dieu." I hear his startled voice as Lars approaches him to lead him to the elevator. I see his legs stiffen and hear his heels click together as he gives a slight formal bow. "I hope you will not regret this decision Monsieur."

"Good night."

I lay there against his body that is tense with anger. But not at me. At least I think it's not at me. I'm confused. I should have listened more carefully when they spoke. Had M. Lafouche offered to buy me? Wanted to borrow me? For himself? For another client?

His heart is loud beneath my ear. I hear the big breath he pulls in rush into his lungs. I feel the tension slowly ease beneath me as I hear the air leave his body. Whatever it had been he had said no. He had protected me.

I slip a finger beneath his top button and work it loose. I stroke the coarse hair on his chest lightly. He lets me and I grow bolder and undo another button. I like the feel of the curly thick hair beneath my fingers. I rarely get to stroke or caress him. His hand covers mine and I stop. It's over already. I peek upwards through my lashes but his head is back on the arm and I cannot see his expression. We stay just like that for a long time and then he takes me to my room.

I feel like something important has happened but I don't know what it is and I lay sleepless for a long time.

I feel a little braver the next day and after he leaves I follow Lars on his rounds. He opens one door after another and nothing happens. The apartment is far larger than I first expected. I see three guest rooms, all with full baths, all done in different colors. I wait outside the blue one when he goes in to dust. I don't like the memories. There's the kitchen, the dining room, the living room, a library, a study, a room filled with weight machines and mats. I feel the blood rush through my veins when Lars shows me an indoor pool. That has to wait until he unclips my bracelets. There is my room and bath and his room and Mister Caldwell's room. Lars doesn't let me into Mister Caldwell's room. It is the only place I am forbidden.

"But why?"

"Mister Caldwell says so." End of conversation.

I help Lars as much as I am able. The bracelets make certain tasks impossible. I'm happy to be doing things and to have someone to talk to. Occasionally I hear the two tones and then Lars lifts me under his arm as if I am a football and carries me to my bed where he attaches me. I hate to hear the lock of my door snick into place now. I feel twice as lonely as I used to. Sometimes I am only there for an hour. Sometimes for the rest of the day.

Lars has been here a week. He is a true mystery. A man of many talents. A man of one mood. I have never seen him other than he always is. I have never seen an impatient gesture or heard an impatient word from him. I have never seen a scowl cross his face even when I know things aren't going the way he wishes. I have never seen him laugh or cry or snarl or heard him raise his voice. He gives one slow smile when something is done for him and then he is back to his regular bland expression.

There seems to be nothing he can't do. I've watched him thread the thinnest piece of thread through the tiniest eye of a needle. His hands are so large I was unable to even see the needle he held. He cooks like a true chef, he cleans and mends and is exceptionally alert though one would never know it from his expression.

He is extremely gentle. impossibly gentle for one so large yet one day I grew angry when he wouldn't answer a question and cursed him. He stood, turned me and gave me a smack on my rear end that sent me flying across the room. It stung like crazy all day. He never said anything but when Mister Caldwell saw my red bottom, he tightened his lips and made it worse with my own hairbrush before buggering me viciously. I cried all night.

As soon as I apologized the next morning, Lars acted like it had never happened. Mister Caldwell remained angry for a week and I was confined to my room. I suffered under his hand nightly. He teased me to distraction and then beat my ass till I was screaming with pain and need. The two feelings seem to go hand and hand and I end up begging for more. I never am quite sure which it is that I'm begging for. I will never utter a curse again in my lifetime.

My heart is beating wildly and I'm finding it hard to breathe. I know something is going to happen the moment Mister Caldwell comes home. He takes my arm and leads me into my room without a word, his fingers tight like they used to be. He strips me and brings me to the shower. He pushes me to my knees and attaches me tightly to the shower wall by both necklace and bracelets. I'm afraid of the glint in his eye. He watches my face intently, forcing me to meet his gaze again and again as I try to lower my eyes. His penis is thrust in front of my face and I obediently open my mouth, gagging a second later as he brutally forces himself to the back of my throat. Tears blind my eyes and I fight for breath around the enlarged shaft in my throat. He's moving with a vigorous rhythm and I can't move my head to get away. I feel his fingers biting cruelly into my scalp as they grab my hair and tighten. I try to open my mouth wider to suck in air but his shaft is filling me. My nose is clogged with tears and I panic thinking I will choke. I close my teeth slightly and my head is rammed back into the wall. The inch of space could have been a foot for all the force I am hit with. My mouth gapes and I choke and moan as he fucks my mouth. I feel his balls hit my chin when he goes especially deep and I gag, the retching sound muffled by his penis. At long last I hear his grunt, feel the spurts hit the back of my throat and I swallow and swallow, praying I won't be sick. I'm gasping for air when he finally leaves me. I can't stop crying. I hear the water run in the sink. I hear the door shut and I'm left there to wonder why.

My knees are sore by the time he returns. He's naked again and I see he already has an erection. I swallow convulsively and wait. "Look at me."

I do. I can barely tilt my head enough to see his face. The necklace bits into the back of my neck. His eyes grab mine and hold them. My breathing shifts as his fingers lightly rub my nipples. "Remember the feeling," he whispers and then pinches them hard. I gasp in pain but a strange twitching centers low and I feel my clit swell and enlarge.

He unclips me and raises me high up. I'm on tiptoe when he attaches my hands to the wall. He licks a nipple and I start to pant. A finger is lightly rubbing my feminine slit, I clench my legs and hear the click of his tongue. I feel metal, extremely thin metal around both ankles and then my legs are pulled apart and the wrists take my weight. I groan. Pain snakes up from my shoulders but the finger is back and lightly stroking me, a tongue flicking my nipples. Pain and pleasure pulse through me. First one, then the other, then together till I can't tell which is stronger. Which I desire more. I'm moaning. I hear my voice pleading. I whimper with need and then I hear his voice again. "Remember the feeling. Remember the feeling." The whisper reaches me over and over as the intensity builds and builds till I'm screaming with need and then the scream shifts to one of pain as he takes my tender bud and pinches it, the scream changing to one of ecstasy a second later as I gush, my body spasming over and over. I'm spent and hang from my bonds. I can hardly catch my breath. His tongue runs over my nipples lightly. His finger finds its way back to the sensitized organ and I whimper. It is too tender but he continues. My arms and shoulders ache. I feel the metal cutting into my wrists from my weight pulling on them.

He turns on the water and cold hits me, shocking me. I feel it warm gradually and then we are bathed in heat and steam. He bathes, ignoring me. My muscles strain to relieve my wrists. I hear a groan escape my lips. He ignores it.

Soapy hands rub my armpits and pubis. I feel the steady strokes of the razor. His fingers linger and caress. My mouth opens and I suck in warm moist air. I'm almost there and he stops and releases me. I clench my thighs together. My arms are useless for a long minute but he holds me till I can use them. I fight the urge to rub myself against his leg. I want to cry with frustration.

He leads me back to the bedroom and sits on the bed. He pulls me between his legs and sucks my breasts. I can feel my vagina trying to grip what isn't there. His hands push me down and I take his shaft in my mouth. He lays back and I continue a long time till he finally shoots into my mouth. I clean him off and stay still as he remains laying on the bed. I wait. I lean back on my heels and stare at the hair on his legs. His legs are well shaped and muscular. Impressive as long as they aren't next to Lars'. I see his twin sacks slack and hanging, his shrunken penis lying on his hard flat belly. His chest is well developed and rises above his ribs. I can just see the tiny hard nipples peek through the hair. I cannot see his face. I wait.

Time seems to slow to a crawl. I watch his chest rise and fall and wonder if he's asleep. I've never seen him sleep. Does he snore? Does he toss and turn? Does he sleep on his side or back or stomach? I shift my weight and slide my hip to the floor, taking the pressure off my legs. They are stiff and ache. I listen to his quiet breathing. Time seems suspended. My head leans against the side of the bed.

I jerk awake as I feel myself falling. He is sitting again, watching me. I look up nervously but he smiles and runs his finger along my cheek. Such a gentle caress. His hand on my arm lifts me and I stand placid between his legs. The glint is gone from his eye.

He brushes my hair back off my face, his touch light and feathery. I begin to relax. Lips touch my eyes, my lips, my ear. I become languid. His hands caress my neck and shoulders. Thumbs strum my nipples. I am sucking in air. His breath tickles my ear sending shivers of pleasure through me. A tongue glides down my collarbone and fastens onto a turgid nipple. I am liquid. My fingers creep up and glide through his silky hair pressing his head to me. Tongue and fingers work me up to a feverish pitch but never go lower. I ache with need. I hear a soft whimper in the back of my throat and then hands take my shoulders and move me back from him. I open eyes full of lust and see his steady penetrating gaze. I'm disoriented and confused, my feelings shifting back and forth, desire swiftly fading as he turns me and clips my wrists together behind me. What have I done?

He takes a black corset and I step into it. The strings

are drawn very tight. "We'll have to get that instructor here soon darling," he whispers in my ear and gives them another sharp tug. My breath is labored and I feel a moments dizziness as I struggle to get used to the tightness. I hear faint clicks and see him removing two extremely thin bands from my ankles. Stockings slide up my legs followed by garters. The band are put back on. I step into high heels. He hasn't had me dress this way in weeks. My uneasiness grows deep in my belly.

He brushes my hair and then with a practiced twist it is formed into a pompadour and pinned. He teases a tendril or two down and then applies make up to my face expertly.

We eat dinner, my left hand attached to the chair. I'm confused and nervous. I spill my wine when my hand shakes. His eyes keep studying me and I find it hard to swallow without choking. Lars clears the dishes and I sit and wait while he sips his brandy. He hasn't uttered one word during the meal. I stare at the tablecloth. I see him rise out of the corner of my eye and I wait. Fingers lift my chin. His thumb brushes my lips. "Why are you nervous Miss Julia?"

"I don't understand." My voice quivers and I swallow so I won't cry.

"What is there to understand. Did you not promise to serve me? To obey me?"

I nod, wishing he'd let my chin go so I could lower my eyes. "Yes sir."

His thumb puts gentle pressure on my lips and I draw it in and suck lightly. I see his smile. Feel his fingers on my nipples. They harden at once. His smile widens and he removes both hands from me. He reaches down and releases me and leads me to the pillar in front of the elevator. My belly twists with anxiety as he attaches my wrists to each side behind me, my legs on either side keeping them spread slightly. His finger caresses my cheek and moves to my breasts. He teases the nipple so lightly. His other finger tickles my feminine slit and my loins clench. His eyes are so close to mine as he watches my reactions. ''Be a good girl,'' he whispers and then moves away and sits on the couch.

I'm scared and aroused at the same time. I wait knowing what I will hear and not long after the two tones sound. I strain my ears and hear the elevator rising. I'm holding my breath between pants. I can feel perspiration on my upper lip. The doors part and Mrs. Porto steps out. I freeze at the wide smile she gives me.

''Why it is perfect Mister Caldwell,'' she purrs. She approaches me and walks around me. ''The contrast is exquisite. Ultra modern room and a Victorian Miss captive.'' Her hand strokes my neck and I flinch. I see her brows raise in surprise. A thoughtful almost cruel look enters her eyes as she surveys my body. Her hand closes on my breast and I cringe. I feel her squeeze it hard and gasp.

''I don't think your pet likes me stroking her Mister Caldwell,'' she murmurs, turning questioning eyes to my master. I can not see him as he is behind me somewhere. I do not hear him respond. My breath is harsh. My stomach cramping as I tense.

Cool appraising eyes return to my frightened ones. ''I know you are sensitive to touch Miss Julia,'' she whispers, placing a kiss on the hollow of my throat. I try to strain away but cannot move. Her lips linger on my shoulders and work lower.

My head is shaking back in forth in protest. ''No. Don't. Please.'' I hardly recognize the ragged whisper as my own.

I groan as her lips clamp onto a nipple, sucking it in, flicking it with her tongue. I hate myself for the thrill that shoots to my loins. This can't be happening.

It can't be. I strain to close my legs against her invading fingers but it's useless. Her lips are moving from one breast to another and I feel the fire lowering in my belly. Her mouth trails up my neck, her breath is feather light in my ear and then she is probing my mouth with her tongue. I panic.

I hear her scream of pain and feel my cheek burst into fire at the same moment. "You horrid little bitch," she spits out at me, staring at the blood in her hand. I see her eyes narrow and darken. She whips off her sash and leaves my sight. The cloth spreads my lips and digs viciously into my mouth as she ties my head to the post, effectively gagging me. Where is Mister Caldwell? Where is Lars? I'm truly frightened now.

She thrusts her face close to mine. I smell her perfume. "You don't like a woman's touch?" She snorts and flicks a nipple with a sharp nail. My eyes tear with pain. "You don't know what you like yet. You're still being trained. There are many, many things you haven't experienced yet. Some you will like. Some I know you won't," she sneers ominously.

Her hand is between my legs, her expert fingers rolling the tiny, already hard bud. My body keeps shifting from fear to disgust to need. I can't control my frantic thoughts, my building feelings. Her lips suck in a nipple painfully hard. Two fingers delve deep in my love tunnel, the nails catching and hurting, the thumb still circling the engorged knob. I fight my bonds to no avail. How can such thin pieces of gold hold so strongly?

Teeth chew on my nipple and I moan. I can't stop crying and I fear I will choke on my tears. I can barely swallow with the gag so cruelly tight. A finger is thrust up my ass and I scream through the fabric. It's hardly heard.

She leaves me and I open my eyes. She never takes

her eyes from mine and watches me closely as she slowly disrobes. She is shaved as I am. I see the malicious smile that barely lifts the corner of her mouth. Her eyes are narrowed and half closed. She looks like a tiger ready to pounce and devour.

Her hands stroke me and I tense for pain but her touch remains light and feathery. I don't like how my body is shifting gears again. I'd rather the pain which I can fight. Soft fingers stroke my slit. My buttocks are rubbed and caressed, my anus massaged on the outside only. Light nibbles caress my throat. My breathing is tortured. I hate this I tell myself but my senses say differently. She breathes in my ear and I shiver. She rubs her breasts against mine and it titillates me. I feel her shaved mound rotating against mine and I shrink back but she follows and soon I am trying to press against her. Such softness rubbing against it. I feel the hard tiny knob against my own and it makes me jerk as searing heat centers and builds. Her mouth is on my breasts, tonguing, licking, sucking and I'm screaming as the climax takes me over the edge. She continues to rub against me and I feel her body tensing with her own orgasm and then she slows her movements till she finally stops. She leans against me heavily.

After a short time she places a kiss on my neck. I can't meet her eyes. I'm disgusted with myself. Thoroughly humiliated. I hear her amused chuckle. "Remember this. You don't care how you get there. All you want is to get there." I can't look at her.

She fondles my breast. "You're very sensitive to touch little one. It is your downfall. It is what makes you perfect for this. You were meant to be taken and molded. To be shown all the different ways." She leans down and sucks the nipple in slowly, working her tongue around and around and I feel the tightening of my legs. She stands again and lifts my chin. Her eyes mock me. "You respond so well. You like being helpless. You like being told what to do. You like living in a state of anticipation. Of not knowing what might be next." She leans against me and rubs herself lightly against my body. "You owe me little one." Her voice is low and soft, almost caressing. "And I will be paid back. I promise you."

I feel a chill of apprehension tickle my spine. Her words are so soft, her look so hard. Her eyes tell me she is deadly serious. I watch her dress and then leave through the elevator doors. I'm left there a long time and then Lars releases me and takes me to my room. My mouth is sore. He won't speak to me. He removes my shoes, stockings and corset. He pulls down my hair and pulls me into the bathroom. my pleas to use the toilet are ignored and I'm attached to a hook in the ceiling. It's the first time I'm suspended and the pain is terrible. I cry and plead but he leaves. Surely my shoulders will be pulled out of joint.

I don't hear Mister Caldwell enter. I hear the swish of the riding crop and feel the bite of the lash. I kick and scream but it just causes more pain. He seems to go on forever and I reach a state where the pain begins to dissolve and it becomes something else. Something unexplainable that is both frightening and exciting. Something I dread but want. Something I fear but look forward to.

I collapse when he takes me down. I cannot sit for two days. I am locked in my room. Lars brings me food. I don't see Mister Caldwell. I don't care but lay there and cry in self-pity. Something has changed again. I have less thoughts of leaving. I can feel how I am slowly letting him take over my life. I am beginning to accept what he tells me.

I am kept with my wrists clipped, usually behind me. Mister Caldwell is cold and distant. I'm wracked with guilt that I have disappointed him again. He makes no attempt to arouse me. He comes in each night and bends me over and buggers me hard and deep. No soft caresses. No wonderful smile. He knows I hate it. I'm starting to feel I deserve the punishment.

He comes to me a few mornings later. It is the first time he has come in the morning since Mrs. Porto was here. I watch him warily but he smiles and I relax. We shower and he shaves me. I kneel when he pushes my shoulders and I take him in my mouth. I'm ridiculously grateful for this gesture of forgiveness. I almost cry when I feel the soft caress of his finger on my cheek. I grab his hand and kiss it. I love him. I'll do anything for him.

He leads me into the bedroom and i step into a small piece of stretchy black spandex. He slides it up and it forms a sort of Y. The material is about three inches wide and comes to my waist where it separates into two strips that cover my breasts. Just. The strips meet again at the back of my neck and become narrower so they end in a thong between my cheeks and meet the other half between my legs. i look at him questioningly but he ignores it and clips my bracelets together in front of me.

We eat in silence. I hear the two tones while we sit but he doesn't even look curious. Lars passes the table to answer the summons and I feel my belly twist. I hate when the elevator comes. Mister Caldwell continues to sip his coffee. Lars returns alone and I finally relax.

Mister Caldwell rises and beckons me to him. I walk

around the table and join him. He looks steadily at me and I'm thrown again when that wonderful smile spreads his lips. He takes my arm and we walk down to his weight room. There is a man there. An Asian.

He bows but not before I see the surprised lift of his brows at the sight of my linked hands. "This is your aerobics instructor. Mr. Su."

I nod and look closely at the man. He is my height and thin. The sinewy kind of thin that belies the steel muscles below the skin. His hair is almost shaved but black. His eyes are calculating and assessing as he takes me in. I see his eyes constantly drawn to my bracelets.

"You do as he says," Mister Caldwell orders and unclips me. I watch him leave and feel a shudder of apprehension run through me when I turn back and see a sly smile before it leaves Mr. Su's face.

He approaches me and studies me. Walking around me. I feel his hand on my buttocks and flinch. He pinches the skin. "Too loose," he says and comes in front of me. "Stand straight."

I do but look over his shoulder. His eyes unnerve me. He runs his hand over my belly, grabs flesh at my waist. Prods my breasts. He pinches the skin on the underside of my arm. I don't move. I won't meet his eyes. Lars is here, I keep telling myself.

He starts music and I follow his lead, hearing his barking voice whenever I miss a step. I stretch and turn and move. My muscles complain quickly. I have had no exercise in months. How long? I wonder and miss a step. I feel a sting on my thigh and quickly concentrate again. The first session is short. Only twenty minutes but I'm exhausted and out of breath when it's over. Lars comes for me and escorts Mr. Su to the elevator. He bows and the big man nods. I get the feeling Lars doesn't care for Mr. Su.

Lars turns and leaves for the kitchen and I feel deserted and vulnerable. I wander around and end up back in the kitchen with the giant. "Can you teach me to make some of the delicious dishes you make?"

He shrugs and continues to shred lettuce. "Ask Mister Caldwell."

"Would you?"

"No." End of conversation. I sigh and sit watching him. I can feel the perspiration tickling down between my breasts.

"Can I take a shower?" When is the last time I bathed myself?

I see the shake of his head and sigh again. I hear the two tones and glance quickly at Lars. He's watching me steadily. I rise and hold out my hands to him but he walks past me, stopping at the door. "Sit."

I do. Quickly. He leaves and I watch the door swing to and fro in surprise. I don't know what to do. I've never been out of my room when an unexpected person comes up. Maybe Lars knows who it is? Maybe this is a test? Maybe I could just peek? Maybe I better not.

I sit and wait.

I hear voices. Lars' and another male's but I can't recognize it. I strain my ears. I'm dying to peek. I'm terrified of getting caught. My heart is pounding in my chest. I get up and sit right back down. I wait.

Lars returns not a moment later. He studies my face and then goes back to the salad. I lick my lips. "Who was that?"

Silence.

He finishes the salad and picks up a plate. "Can I eat in here with you?" I ask hesitantly. He stops and again studies my face. I feel I've made a major gaffe and lower my eyes. The plate slides onto the table into my line of sight. I look up quickly and see the fleetingest lift of a lip. "Thank you Lars," I whisper and he sits down and we eat in companionable silence.

I start to clear my plate but one lift of his brow stops me. "I just want something to do," I say quietly with a shrug, wincing as my sore muscles protest. I sit there and watch him for a while and then rise to return to my room.

"Miss Julia sit down," he says with his back still towards me. I do but I'm puzzled. I wait knowing it will do no good to ask. He wipes the counter and then approaches me, crooking his finger for me to follow him.

We return to the weight room and I groan thinking he wants me to start working with weights today. He begins to undress and I take a hasty step backward. I see the slightly hurt look that flashes in his eyes and immediately feel guilty. I stand partly in awe, partly in terror as each part of his body is revealed. He beckons me to him and I have to swallow before I can force my feet to move. I refuse to let my eyes look lower than his neck.

His hands descend to my shoulders and the spandex is peeled from my body in one swift movement. I feel the blood leave my face and sway slightly. His fingers tighten on my shoulders and I open my eyes and try to blink the tears from them.

"Lars does not lie Miss Julia. I would take no pleasure in ruining you." I nod quickly, trying to stop shaking as I hear his words. He picks me up as if I were an infant and throws me over his shoulder with a, for him, light smack to my rear. We leave the weight room and then I'm flying through the air before hitting water and sinking. The coolness closes over me and I gulp in liquid, struggling to get to the surface, spluttering and choking when I do. I turn and see Lars' huge body hurtling towards me as he cannonballs off the diving board. I give a screech of terror and then find myself lifted and pushed against the side by the force of the wave he creates. He surfaces and I hear his laugh for the first time. It's surprisingly high for someone of his size. "Feels good doesn't it?" he asks and then starts swimming laps. I tread water and watch him till he stops and beckons me to him. "Swim. It's good for the muscles."

I do but not like him. He swims two sometimes three laps to my one, his grin as he passes me each time making me try to swim faster but I'm no match for him and give up quickly. I feel the muscles loosening as I stroke back and forth and eventually I just turn over and float. It's delicious. I bob along, more quickly every time Lars passes me till he passes and grabs my leg as he goes, dragging me under the water for a few feet. I surface to see his face wreathed in smiles, his laughter echoing in the enclosed room. I can't help but join him. I suddenly feel light and free and find myself wishing Mister Caldwell were here to enjoy this with us.

I follow Lars out of the pool and he lifts me onto a table by the wall. "Lie down on your belly." I do and wait. Wet hair is brushed aside. Oil trickles onto my back and those huge hands start massaging and digging deliciously into my flesh. My neck, shoulders, spine, buttocks, legs. Everything turns to liquid under his manipulations. I feel myself turned and he starts again at my neck. The hands are sure and purposeful. The fingers probe and rub and dig and pull. Muscle after muscle obeys his demand for them to relax and I'm as weak as a kitten when he reaches my feet again. I feel a cool sheet wrapped around me and arms lifting me and I am asleep before we reach my room.

I am home with my mother and she is soothing me gently. I feel her fingers stroking my arm. I'm safe. I'm protected. I sigh and stretch. I see Mister Caldwell looking down at me and give him a lazy smile, still wrapped up in my dreams. He gives me a small smile in return.

"You're lazy today."

"I had a nice day today," I murmur shyly. I notice Mister Caldwell is nude at the same time I feel the sheet tugged loose from my body. He lifts it and stares down at my white, oily flesh, a slow smile curving his lips. For some reason I blush and he chuckles.

"Are you still modest Miss Julia? Have I not taught you well enough?"

"Yes sir." I'm nervous. I don't like the way he's looking at me. It's too intense. His eyes capture mine and I'm locked into his gaze. I feel his finger tracing a line down from my neck. My heart quickens and I hold my breath, waiting for it to reach my nipple. I feel my nipples crinkle in anticipation. He slows and watches me. His finger stops directly between my breasts. I know he can feel my heart thumping. I know he sees the pulse in my neck beating frantically. His eyes darken and my heart picks up an even faster pace.

"So slippery," he murmurs and lays down on top of me in the missionary position.

Things shift and I'm disoriented. I don't know what to do with my hands. My hands have never been free during sex. I lay quietly beneath him. He kisses my lips, eyes, back to my lips. His breath tickles my ear. I'm panting. He grinds his hips and our bodies slide easily, the oil on mine lubricating us both. His chest hair rubs and teases my sensitive nipples. A tongue flicks out and traces a path down my neck. I'm awash in sensation. I raise my hands and put them tentatively on his arms. I can feel the hairs beneath my fingers and rub them lightly. I like touching him. I love him touching me. He slips into me and pumps gently, slowly, deeply. I spread my legs further and match his movements. His tongue is in my mouth, searching, arousing. My hands move to his shoulders and I feel the muscles bunch and move beneath them. The build up is slow, steady, but so exquisite. He has only made love to me this way once before and then my hands had been held. My arms hold him tight to my body as I feel the sensations meld and blossom. I rub myself against him as hard as I can and then it bursts and flows and I hold him and cry at the beauty of it. His low grunt mingles with the sound of my sobs. Warm lips kiss the tears from my cheeks. His body shifts and he lays next to me, pulling me tight against his side and he lets me cry till I finish on my own. I feel so at peace. So loved.

"I'm sorry," I whisper, knowing how he hates tears. His arm tightens slightly but he says nothing. I am content to lay against him, my hand on his chest. I so rarely am allowed to touch him, to stroke his skin. I love the tightness, the smoothness of his body. I love the coarseness of his body hair.

I love him.

We shower and I feel hurt when he attaches me to the wall. I had foolishly thought it wouldn't happen anymore. He washes my hair and soaps me up, turning me to get my back. The water rinses me and I feel his lips on my neck.

"I hear you were a good girl today Miss Julia." A thrill races through me and and I stay still waiting. "Good girls deserve a surprise."

He leads me out of the shower and clips my wrists behind me. He pushes me onto a small seat in the corner and leaves, closing the door. My heart is thudding with excitement. When he returns he is in a three piece suit.

Brushing and drying my hair seem to take a lifetime. I'm too keyed up to enjoy the tug of the bristles and he jerks my hair more than once in warning to remain still. I try. I don't dare do anything to ruin. . . . . what? I have always found the waiting the hardest and this is driving me insane.

My hair is finally in its usual style and he holds out a white corset for me to step into. White stockings, beautiful embroidered white garters and white heels. My make up seems to take longer than usual tonight or is it just that I'm heady with anticipation?

He releases my hands and leads me into the bedroom and I give an exclamation of delight. A dress, a real dress, lies on the foot of the bed. I rush to it, feeling the softness between my fingers. It is white, some sort of soft flowing material and a real dress. I have to blink rapidly to stop the happy tears.

He takes it and I step into it. It's Victorian style except for the length. The collar is high and buttons up my neck. The sleeves are tight and to the wrist. A soft overlay of lace down the front is the only thing that hides my breasts from full view though a faint suggestion of the darker nipples can be seen. It hugs my waist tightly and falls to mid calf. It moves with me. I twirl and watch the skirt settle around my legs. "Thank you,'' I whisper, trying hard to keep my happy tears in control.

My chin is lifted. I feel the light touch of his lips and then I feel his hands on my hair. I turn and look in the mirror. A wide brimmed hat is perched becomingly on my head. It is white and finished with chiffon. I could have stepped out of a magazine page from a hundred years ago.

I turn questioning eyes toward Mister Caldwell but he takes my arm and leads me out. Lars is at the elevator and my heart gives a lurch of fear. I hate when the elevator comes up. I'm shaking and confused when Mister Caldwell walks past the pillar. Everything seems to shift and move slowly. I can't grasp what is happening. Lars places a beautiful white shawl over my shoulders and the doors open. The elevator is empty. This somehow seems more ominous and I pull back when Mister Caldwell tries to take me into it. I feel a rasping in my throat, a soft finger on my cheek. ''Easy.'' His voice is low. Soothing. I can't stop shaking.

I flinch as the doors close and make a wild grab for Mister Caldwell's hand when he lets go of my arm. I'm terrified. I want to be back in my room. He disengages my clutching fingers and holds my hands tightly and I immediately feel more secure. This is known.

''Look at me Miss Julia.'' I do and his gaze holds me. I feel my heart slowing down. My wrists are tight in his one hand and his other lifts and strokes my cheek. He cups my chin and kisses my lips. ''I will stay with you,'' he whispers and I let out a shaky sigh of relief.

Had that been the unknown fear? Abandonment? Aloneness?

The doors open and he takes my arm. I have to force myself to put one foot in front of another. I see people rushing by the glass doors. Sam appears on the other side of the glass and opens it as we approach.

I'm hit with noise and movement at once. I freeze. People rush past me, cars and buses fly by, brakes squeal, horns blare. The air vibrates with movement and noise as if it has a life of its own. It seems to be surrounding me, devouring me. Everything seems to be coming at me and I panic and try to step back but Mister Caldwell's arm stops me. "Easy," he murmurs, pulling me toward the open limousine door.

Sam is at the car door, smiling at me but I'm numb. One foot follows the other and then I'm in the small, dim interior and I feel better immediately. The door shuts after Mister Caldwell and the outside sounds are muted. I sit and shake. I want to go back home. Home?

An arm around my shoulders draws me close to his body. I can't seem to stop shaking. It is too much. It's been too long. His hand soothes my cheek. His breath caresses my ear before his tongue licks the lobe gently. Things shift once more and the outside world slowly dissolves until it completely disappears. His hand toys with my breasts beneath the lace overlay. The nipples respond to him as always. My legs clench as my loins start to pulsate with desire. A thumb traces my jaw line, my collarbone. Small circles around my breast leave me breathless.

"Just concentrate on the feelings," he whispers and gives me one more kiss. I feel the car stop and hear Sam get out. Everything shifts once more and I take a deep breath to try to steady myself. I take Mister Caldwell's hand and step out into a different atmosphere. It is quieter. Cooler. Night is almost upon us and the light is diminishing quickly. I feel better.

We enter a restaurant that is dim and quiet. A gentle murmur of voices, an occasional burst of laughter, the soft clink of china. It is reassuring. The Maitre D' approaches us and greets Mister Caldwell familiarly. He leads us to a table where two men are already seated.

My breath catches in my throat. The men stand and I lower my eyes as they openly appraise me.

"This is Miss Julia," Mister Caldwell introduces and I nod at their greeting. I'm not told their names. Mister Caldwell seats me and I clasp my hands in my lap. I can't bring myself to look up. I'm afraid of the looks I might see.

Their voices swirl around me but I hear no words. I stare at the empty plate before me. I wish I was back home in my room. I'm uncomfortable with so many people around me. I seem to have lost the ability to socialize. I cannot think of one thing to say. I swallow and feel the high collar around my neck. It suddenly seems to be tightening. I tug at it and feel my hand clasped in his.

"Do you need to go to the ladies room Miss Julia?"

I raise startled eyes to his steady ones. They are studying me closely. My eyes flick around the restaurant and I feel the beginnings of panic. I can't walk across the room by myself. I don't know where it is. I shake my head hastily and feel my fingers kissed and released.

"Your companion is beautiful." The silky words strike terror in me. I don't want to be admired by any but Mister Caldwell. M. Lafouche had admired me. I feel my hands start to shake and quickly clasp them together.

"My little pet is lovely is she not," Mister Caldwell says quietly. I know he is looking at me and I feel the color rise in my cheeks. Do the men know what he means or do they think it an endearment. I can't make myself look up to see their expressions.

Dinner is served and I eat mine slowly, carefully chewing each bite so I won't choke. I drink my wine, my eyes raising once and catching the heavier man staring at me. I almost spill it. I have to wait a while before I trust myself to lift the glass again.

I have no idea what I eat. I have no conception of time passing. I just am. And as always waiting.

Mister Caldwell rising, startles me out of my stupor. I jerk to my feet, afraid he plans to leave me with the men. He smiles knowingly and caresses my cheek. "We're not leaving yet Miss Julia. Just our guests."

I blush at my gauche behavior and seat myself slowly. I nod when the men say their farewells. Have I embarrassed him? Is he angry with me? Why did he bring me?

I feel his hand on my arm and rise obediently. We walk into another room. It is darker. Small tables are spaced widely apart to insure privacy. A fire burns in the great fireplace against a far wall. Soft candlelight bathes the room. It is an intimate room. He seats me at the most distant table. A waiter appears shortly and places two cordials on the table.

I watch his face in the candlelight as he hands me one of the glasses. "Did you enjoy my surprise?"

"Yes sir." I sip the liqueur. It is sharp and tangy. Minty. Cool and hot at the same time.

His eyes watch me and it unnerves me. I try to smile but I can feel the stiffness in my face. "Why did you think I was leaving Miss Julia? Didn't I tell you I would stay with you?" His voice is low, expressionless. I cannot tell if he's angry.

"I'm sorry. I wasn't paying attention and when you stood it startled me."

"You thought I was leaving."

"I'm sorry." My voice is small, almost a whimper. I feel the uneasiness settling into my belly. He's being too persistant. He is angry.

We finish the liqueurs and he rises. I wait not looking at him. I stare at the candle flickering in the middle of the table and see him move out of my line of sight. My breathing is rapid. I hear the soft murmur of other's voices. The clink of ice hitting the sides of glasses. The occasional ping of glasses clinking together. I can hardly breath. He wouldn't leave me here would he? I can't work up the courage to turn and look. I swallow. My hands clasp each other hard.

I continue to stare at the candlelight. Another liqueur appears on the table before me. I see the white cuff sticking out of the black sleeve of the waiter's jacket as he places the glass. Only one glass. In front of me. I bite my lower lip and fight the threatening tears but they win and leak from my eyes. I lower my head so no one will see. I can barely swallow around the lump in my throat. I have no idea of what to do.

A finger brushes my wet cheek and another lifts my chin. I see a blurry outline in the dim light. "Finish your cordial Miss Julia. Sam is waiting."

I suck in a ragged breath and nod miserably. He is angry. The liquid burns my throat and I choke slightly. I rise when he moves my chair back. His fingers take my arm and he leads me outside. The air has turned cool and I shiver. It's the beginning of fall I realize suddenly. So much time has passed. The shawl is re-arranged around my shoulders. I huddle into its warmth.

It's a silent ride, his fingers absently stroking my hand that lays on his lap. I try to relax but the hat and corset both keep me upright and stiff. I cannot lounge or put my head back. It makes burying ones fears that much harder.

The street is almost deserted when we pull up to his building. We enter the lobby. I see the key inserted. The door opens and we are ascending. Lars is at the top to greet us. He takes my shawl. Pulls out the hat pin and removes my hat. I'm led to my bedroom, pushed over the footboard, arms clipped wide, stretched and skirt lifted up. My breathing has been tortured since the elevator doors opened. He makes me wait for it. I can feel the air on my exposed buttocks. I tense and clench. I don't know if he's in the room. The silence is absolute. I feel the blanket beneath my cheek. Another sign that Autumn is arriving.

Fingers touch my slit and I suck in air. They tease and torment till I'm digging one knee into the back of the other. I hear the click of a tongue. Feel my legs pulled apart and silky loops tightening. The thick belt hits me unexpectedly and I yelp. The second blow lands immediately and I barely draw a breath to scream before the third comes down with a sickening crack. My breath rushes out of me and I struggle to breathe. Blows fall one after another, fingers pull and rub and then my screams hit a different note. He leaves me there all night.

Lars comes to me in the morning and helps me into my leotard. I'm served breakfast in my room. I miss Mister Caldwell. I want to apologize. He's already gone when we go to the weight room.

I'm instructed on the use of the machines and Lars keeps me at it all morning. My muscles are stiff and store from being stretched out all night. He ignores my pleas to stop but makes me continue. I hate it. I'm not allowed to go in the pool. I'm not given a massage. I'm taken to my room and left. I wish I had the nerve to give myself a shower. I don't dare. I don't even remove the leotard. I wait.

He enters silently, as always. I find myself blushing again under his intense stare. I fall to my knees in front of him but he ignores me. I hastily rise and follow him.

His hands are rough as they remove my leotard. He's still angry. "I'm sorry," I whisper but he ignores it. I'm pushed into the shower, stretched, shaved, turned, soaped and then bent all the way over. He's vicious in his movements and I throb with pain. He leaves and I cry as I stand between the drying panels. There's a tray in my room. I miss him.

Every other day Mr. Su comes and gives me my aerobic lesson. Every session he gets more confident. His fingers prod more, slip more as he places me in certain positions. I was told to obey him. I make no complaint. I feel the slight rubbing against my body as he leans over me to instruct me on movement. His smacks come faster and more frequently. They are steadily growing in strength. I know Lars sees my red thighs and bottom when he massages me but nothing is said. Does he think they are from Mister Caldwell? Some of them are.

My body is firming and toning. I feel more alive and supple than I have in a very long time. I glow with pride when Mister Caldwell remarks he can take the corset in another inch. It is worth all the effort to feel his soft kiss on my neck.

We are eating dinner in the dining room. Lars is eating with us which is unusual. I listen to them discussing a small dinner party that Mister Caldwell is giving tomorrow. It sounds as if some very important persons will be coming. I feel a knot beginning to form in my belly. It hardens when I see his speculative gaze on me. I drop my eyes but his hand on mine makes them rise again.

"You will attend tomorrow." The words should

thrill me but his look and tone frighten me. His eyes are too intense. I see the thoughtful glint in them that always means he's wondering if I will obey something he'll desire me to do. I feel my limbs start to shake. I eat the rest of my meal automatically.

We spend the rest of the night on the couch, his voice rolling over me as he reads to me. One hand holds the book, his other strokes and caresses my breasts. I clench my thighs but stop at the warning pinch my nipple gets. I'm going crazy with desire. He hand stops. It starts. I'm panting.

I jump when the book snaps shut. I'm pushed lightly to the floor. I don't need to ask. I unzipper him and take him in my mouth. He sighs. Lars walks into the room and asks about champagne amounts. I don't skip a beat. I'm lifted and he sits on the couch. I stand on the seat and his tongue sears into my slit. I can barely control my trembling legs. I'm pulled down onto his stiff shaft and I ride him. I'm lifted off, turned, penetrated from the rear, his penis deep in my vagina. I hump back against him. He pulls out, penetrates my ass, I don't care and still hump back against him. I'm liquid with need.

He pulls from me and lays flat. I'm straddling him on all fours. My cunt is inches from his mouth. His penis is directly in front of me. I swallow, knowing what he wants. I can't. I must. I swallow again and feel the retch building. I shake my head and gag. His fingers penetrate my ass and begin moving. My head lowers slightly as sensation overtakes me. A flick of his tongue, a gentle pressure on my back, lips on my clit and I lower my mouth over his shaft. I brush my teeth and rinse out my mouth ten times that night.

Mister Caldwell enters my room earlier than usual the next morning. I'm allowed to go to the bathroom and brush my teeth and then he watches me eat my breakfast. I'm nervous. His look is impatient and calculating at the same time. He beckons and I go to him. His eyes rove my naked body. His touches a nipple and it hardens immediately. I see his pleased smile. He strokes me. Kisses my neck, my eyes, my lips. Shivers of pleasure caress my body. He leads me to the bed. I'm spread-eagled and attached. He strokes me a long time and I'm crazy with need. He kisses my lips, puts a piece of tape across my mouth and leaves. I'll surely go mad.

It takes a long time for my congested loins to ease and the feeling to dissipate. I can only assume there are people in the apartment and he's not willing to take a chance with me.

What would I do if given a choice? Would I flee? Do I want to?

No. I don't. I love him. I want to please him. I need him. This has become my whole world. What would I do outside? Who would take care of me? Where did the independent young girl go that could take care of herself and was going to conquer the world? Who cares.

I have to tell him. The thought leaves as quickly as it forms. He already knows. He knew before I did. I'm bound here because he wants it that way. Because he has made me want it to be that way. It will always be as he wants it.

He enters at lunch time, strokes me, coaxes me to moan with want and then releases me. I can hardly swallow my sandwich as he watches me eat. His silence is so total sometimes.

I'm reattached, stretched, stroked, yearning and then he replaces the tape and leaves. How can I love such a man?

I'm given a light dinner and then we shower. He washes me over and over, taking me to the edge again and again. I'm whimpering, begging and he finally brings me to orgasm. I suck him there in the shower, the hot water pounding my neck and shoulders, the steam enveloping and caressing us. I hear his grunt and swallow expertly. He leans back against the door and I hold his shrinking member in my mouth till he moves and it dislodges. I'm lifted up, kissed, stroked, licked. I need him again but he leads me out and we stand in between the partition of warm air. I want to be held, to feel his body rub against mine but he makes no move to touch me.

Can I reach out to him? No. It isn't allowed.

He rubs rose scented lotion all over me. I melt under the touch. I can hardly sit still as he blow dries my hair and arranges it. He tucks two rose buds on the side of the bun. Tendrils are pulled and teased into place.

I step into black stockings. Elaborately embroidered red garters are pulled into place. A black satin and lace corset is pulled around me and tightened. It has two tiny rosebuds that sit between my bare breasts. They seem to enhance how white my skin is. How long since I felt sunlight on me? I have no idea.

I slide my feet into the ridiculously high heels and

watch Mister Caldwell's appraising eyes. I relax when he smiles. "Do you approve?" I ask tentatively.

"You wouldn't leave the room till I did," he answers seriously. He puts on my make up. My lips turn scarlet under the gloss he rubs into them. He darkens my eyes with liner and puts the lightest amount of blush on my cheeks.

I stand at his touch and he turns me, clipping my wrists tightly together. My belly twists. I watch him go to the cabinet and my legs begin to tremble. He looks inside for a long moment and then shuts the door and returns. He has a wide black satin mask in his hands. It looks like the elaborate eye masks people wear to fancy dress balls but this has no eye holes.

"These men wouldn't be comfortable if you could recognize them later," he says, slipping the mask over my eyes. I can feel the stiff arms of the mask sliding through my hair and then tightening. It won't come off easily. Hands stroke my breasts. Lips. Tongue. My breath quickens.

I'm led forward, pushed face down and feel the bed under my upper half. I wait. My heart is pounding. I lick dry lips. I hate the silence the thick carpeting insures. I hear the scratchy sound of a jar unscrewing and I clench. The sting is instantaneous. I try to relax. "This is for your own good pet." His voice is next to my ear. I hear and feel his breath. It tickles. It excites. A thin tube enters my anus and I feel something strange. "Relax," he whispers. The tube is removed.

I've been oiled.

He pulls me upright and I feel his fingers smoothing strands of hair into place. More lipstick. I don't blot it tonight. My lips must look moist. He leads me out and I feel my arms drawn tightly behind me as he attaches me to the pillar. There is a little slack to the chain. My legs are left free. My heart is pounding. Fear? Anticipation? Excitement?

I hear the two tones and hold my breath. "Relax." His voice is so low, so close and then I hear the doors opening.

Greetings are exchanged. Something sounds vaguely familiar about one of the men's voices. I strain my ears. I can't remember. I hear the delighted laugh of one. "How charming." I flinch at a touch of my nipples. Whose?

"I've heard of men who have pets but have never met one before." His hand is stroking me slowly as if feeling his way over unknown territory. My leg is touched and I open it wider. I hear a satisfied chuckle. "Delightful."

The sound of voices moves away. They must be in the living room. "Turn to your right Miss Julia." I obey him, hear the appreciative murmurs as I move and am once more in their sight. My hands are tight behind the pillar and it thrusts my chest out. I try to imagine what I must look like. It's hard to think about.

Time seems to drag. Every so often I feel a touch. A brush of a finger. A tongue. A hand caresses my buttocks. I hear a low chuckle. My belly is twisting. I try not to clench. My heart is racing.

I hear Lars' voice behind me. "Dinner is served." His hands undo my bracelets and he leads me forward blindly. I hear a door open and he turns me. Pressure on my shoulders makes me sit down. I feel padded leather under my naked backside. My legs are spread and I hear the anklets clipped onto something. He takes my arms above my head and pulls me backwards and down. My arms are pulled tight above my head and I am clipped into place. I'm laying on my back completely spread and accessible. I wait.

I don't hear them until they are inside the room. "This is wonderful," one murmurs.

"She looks like a tart and a demure virgin at the same time." I hear a sigh. "Sometimes I hate being married."

My chin is taken and my head turned. "Put those red lips to work love." I feel the hard knob and open my mouth. I hear his sigh of pleasure. Fingers stroke my breasts. I feel him lean over me, his tongue teases my nipples. Hands are massaging my buttocks. A finger enters my slit. Another slides into my anus and I hear a hoot of delighted laughter. "She's been well prepared," he cries as his finger massages my insides. I feel nothing.

The penis is drawn from my mouth. "What a shame there's so much disease around," he grunts and I feel his gism hit my chest. He rubs it into my breasts. I hear the crackle of a plastic package being opened. "Safety first he insists," the man says in a tight voice. I feel the rubbery penis enter me and begin to plow deep.

A wet cloth wipes my chest and breasts. A warm mouth sucks and nibbles at their peaks. The penis is withdrawn and I feel him searching for the other opening. The position isn't good and I groan with pain as he forces himself into me. "Don't ruin her. I want a shot at back there," the other says and then slips his slack penis back into my mouth. I try not to moan. I try not to clench against the hurtful intruder. I fail at both.

He gives a deep thrust and I tighten my lips just slightly. They gape wide open as I suck in breath a moment later when he slaps my breasts hard. I've never been struck on the breast before and I can't believe the pain. It is far worse than a belt on my ass. Tears start and I moan. I hear the grunt of one, the disgusted voice of the other. "I can't trust her with you in her ass. All I need is teeth marks on my dick for my wife to see."

The tube is pulled out and I hear a satisfied sigh. The sound of plastic reaches my ear and then the other is jamming my cunt full of his meat. He's angry and rough and I clench as tightly as possible, wanting to speed him on his way to finishing. It feels like it takes forever.

Silence.

Large hands unhook me. Lars. I breathe easier. I'm led forward. I have to blink against the light when he removes my mask. I'm in an unfamiliar bathroom. I look at him but he proceeds to remove my clothes and doesn't utter a word. He turns on the shower, releases my hair and gives me a push into the warm water. I stand there stupidly till he finally speaks.

"Wash yourself thoroughly Miss Julia."

I'm slow and awkward. I rarely do this for myself. I see Lars return with a white shift. My belly twists. The men aren't done with me.

He beckons me out and I obey. I seem to be moving in another dimension. This doesn't really happen to people. Why would anyone share someone they love with someone else? Why do I assume he returns my love? The thought frightens me. I won't think of it.

My hair is blown dry and brushed. I step into the shift and those huge hands deftly button up the tiny buttons till just below my breasts. I see his eyes linger on the redness of the throbbing breast. I see his lips tighten almost imperceptively. The ends hang down enticingly. The nipples just covered. He pulls the shift to my waist, puts me over his knee and I feel the small tube inserted into my tight canal. I can't help but clench. No sting follows, just low words. "Easy Miss Julia."

I'm lifted up and look in the mirror. My hair is long

and straight. I'm barefoot. I could be about fourteen years old. A silky black blindfold blocks out the image.

I'm led back into the room, my wrists attached to each other and then I hear the chink of a chain. A soft snick and my hands are drawn up above my head. I don't hear him leave. I assume he left. I don't hear them return.

"Well isn't this charming." Why does that voice sound so familiar? It is low with a twang to it. I know I should recognize it.

"She looks like a Victorian Miss that needs discipline."

"All women need to be disciplined. They just don't accept it anymore. I curse my father's generation for letting those damn suffragettes get their way. Their husbands should have kept them home and beaten some sense into them."

I feel my arms lower as the chain is unhooked and then I'm over a knee, the other leg firmly over my thighs holding them down. The blood rushes to my face as I hang down. The slap is strong and swift. I jerk and yelp. His hand begins a steady rhythm and my backside heats up fast. I'm panting and moaning. I scream when flesh is exchanged for leather and my mouth is covered. A foot stands on the chain between my wrists and keeps me down easily. I'm writhing and crying, the sounds muted and useless against the hand over my mouth. I can feel his raging hard on beneath me.

It finally ends and I'm dumped onto the floor when he stands. I lay twisting and turning, trying desperately to relieve the incessant stinging. "God damn that felt good. I haven't enjoyed myself so much for a long time. Wish the hell I could do that to my wife sometimes."

"I know just what you want. Mine'd never tolerate it though. Won't even go down on me."

They talk as if I don't exist and then hands pick me up and I'm bent over the bed. My wrists are stretched and I hear the soft clicks. Plastic crinkles, I hear a faint snapping sound. Thank God for the oil. They are ruthless. One after the other. "Let's make it last. My wife would never allow this," the twang chuckles. They take turns. A few pumps by one, then the other. They use me endlessly. No attempt is made to arouse me. I don't exist as a person. I'm just there. Am I there?

They take swipes at my already sensitive rear, laughing when I jerk and groan. A gag is placed in my mouth and they pull out and beat my buttocks some more. I've gone past the pain now. I just exist. I'm hardly aware of it when they place me on top of one of them and the other climbs on my back. My shift is ripped off, my breasts are mauled and sucked. They finally match each other's rhythm and grunt and groan as they exclaim how good it feels to be able to feel each other's penis doing the same thing at the same time in almost the same place. "This is the life Steve," the one on the bottom whispers with a sigh as he comes.

Steve. Steve Cochran. Past president of the United States. All time family man. A pillar of society.

I'm left alone for the next two days. Lars brings me my food and attaches me at night. I don't see Mister Caldwell. I don't exercise. I don't know if I could.

My body is no longer numb. It pulses with feeling. Soreness, need, shame, need, hate, need, anger, need, loneliness. I miss Mister Caldwell.

He comes on the morning of the third day. I watch him warily. I don't know his mood. He stares at me.

Studies me. He crooks a finger and I go to him. Hand on shoulder. I kneel. I wait.

His hand cups my chin and I look up at him towering over me. A thumb traces my jaw line. My mouth goes slack. I see his small smile. He touches my lips, I suck on his thumb. He lifts me up and I stand before him. His fingers stroke my neck, my breasts. I cannot stop the wince when his fingers hit the bruise on my breast. I see his scowl and hold my breath. My eyes drop before his. "I'm sorry," I whisper. Why should I feel guilty?

Fingers on buttons, thin cotton brushed off my shoulders. I hear the quick intake of breath. I'm afraid to see his expression. Light fingers on the bruise. Hands on my neck, stroking. My cheek, eyes, lips, ears, kissed.

He picks me up and cradles me in his arms. I feel the bed beneath me, the thin cotton tugged below my hips. He lowers himself onto me and makes love to me slowly. Thoroughly. Deliciously. I'd do anything for him.

We shower, he shaves me. I see his eyes keep glancing back to the bruise and I fear his anger. His silence is so menacing at times. We eat and then he leaves. I treasure the soft kiss he places on my cheek before he goes.

Mr. Su arrives shortly after and I spend the morning, stretching, moving, dancing. He's taken to carrying a cane and thinks nothing of hitting me with it if he isn't satisfied. Not hard enough to mark me permanently but the sting is no less for it. He's a hard man to please. I'm always happy to see Lars at the end of each session. I'm now up to one and a half hours four times a week.

Mister Caldwell arrives one day for lunch and eats with me. I've already been showered which is very unusual. I sit and fidget in my shift. I stop when he raises an eyebrow. I can feel something is different. Something is going to happen which usually doesn't. I don't want it to. I like my safe world.

He seems distracted. Tense. It frightens me. I choke on a piece of lettuce and flush under his quizzical gaze. A finger beckons and I rise obediently. Our knees touch. His hands hold my waist lightly. "Tell me."

My breathing quickens. I can't seem to form words. I shake my head helplessly. My shift is lifted, I'm guided over his lap. I try not to tense. I fail. I wait. The sting doesn't come. A hand fumbles beneath me and his shaft glides between my tight thighs. My arms tremble as they support me on the floor. "Squeeze your legs." I do. He moves slowly. A hand alternately pushes down on my rear and releases in time to his pumping. Fingers fumble at the buttons for only a minute and then my shift is torn open. Nipples are stroked and pulled. I hear my breath rasping in my throat. My arms are hardly able to support me. The shaft glides against the hairless dome and the tiniest organ grows and pulses. The hand pushes me down hard and the pumping quickens. I'm there at the same time he is, my moans of pleasure drowning out his last grunt. Fingers stroke and soothe my naked rear. I feel the tips tracing the faint outlines left by Mr. Su's cane. My arms are shaking now and I hear his sigh and then his strong arms are lifting me up off of him. I stand in tattered shift before him. My eyes are still slightly glazed and I barely see his smile.

"Go to your room Miss Julia. I'll join you shortly." I do as I'm told. I sit on the bed and wait. I feel myself starting to doze and then he is there watching me.

I flush and am relieved to see his small smile. He's carrying a mink coat over his arm. I feel my eyes widen in surprise. I raise my hand to stroke it but stop in midair. He nods and I touch the luxurious softness. It's almost blue black and I can't get over the feeling of it. I pet and caress it as if it is a living thing that enjoys my touch.

He places it over the back of a chair and tells me to go wash. I do as he says. I can't help but wonder what the coat means.

He is waiting for me when I emerge. He unpins my hair and brushes it. I love the feeling and revel in the gentle tug of the bristles. Lips on my neck as he brushes the mass to one side. He leaves it down. "Miss Julia."

I turn at the low voice and he beckons to me. I feel my hands clipped together behind me and then his tongue on my nipples, my stomach, my mound. I almost sink to my knees but his hands spreading my thighs prevent it. I groan in frustrations when he leaves me. Silk slides up my legs. Garters are snapped onto the tops. Shoes are pushed on. I stand in stockings and heels before him. He appraises every part of my body. I turn at his signal. I feel the pink blush creep up my body. I wait. I expect the feeling of the corset but instead I feel the softness of rich fur against my body. I look down and see the coat draped over my shoulders. My arms are released and I'm turned. I don't understand.

"I have to work very late tonight. I want you with me." He removes the coat from my shoulders and holds it for me. I slip my arms into it in a trance. The inside is fur like the outside. I am cocooned in sensuous, softness. It strokes and tickles my bare skin. I can't quite make my mind work. His arm leads me towards the elevator. I don't trust the elevator. I try to pull back but he ignores the action and we step inside when the doors open. He buttons the coat from the neck to my knees on the way down. He takes a mink hat from his pocket and places it on my head. I'm clutching his coat tightly but he ignores it.

The doors open and he urges me out. My heart is

racing. I can feel myself starting to sway when I see Sam at the glass doors. I don't want to be outside.

The blast of cold air hits me like a physical blow and I'm shocked at the intensity of it. I shudder violently and his arm is maneuvering me around people and then I'm in the warm interior of the car. Mister Caldwell says something to Sam and then he's beside me and the limousine is moving. I feel his eyes on me and then the seat shifts and he is sitting opposite me.

"You look very fetching in that coat Miss Julia." His words caress me.

"Thank you." My voice is shaky. I want him beside me. I want to touch him. I need the reassurance of his hand on me.

"Unbutton it."

Startled eyes raise to his. I can't help flicking them worriedly to the windows.

"Miss Julia I'm waiting." His voice is low. Too low and I quickly fumble with the buttons. "Open it wide." I do. It slides silkily off of my body. My heart is beating wildly. "Open your legs." I do."Wider." I do. "Very nice."

I sit before him uncomfortably. We stop at a light and I see a bicyclist stop next to the window. Can he see in? I look down. My body is stark white against the blackness of the fur. I feel the pink creep along under the skin. I raise my eyes at the sound of his soft chuckle.

"You still retain a degree of modesty."

"I'm sorry," I whisper, unsure of his mood.

"Don't be. I find it charming," he murmurs, his eyes appraising me. "Button up pet. We're almost there."

I hurry to do as he says and find I have buttoned it wrong. The car stops and I hear his impatient sigh. My hands are brushed out of the way and his deft fingers have me put right in a moment. The door opens and he steps out, offering his hand to me a moment later. Low words are discussed with Sam as I glance around.

We are in an underground garage. Only two other cars are present. It is very dim and cool. I shiver and hug myself tight. I don't like it down here. I step closer to Mister Caldwell. I'm used to the bright rooms of the apartment. I feel better as soon as he takes my arm. We walk down a darker hallway and then he puts a key into a slot next to the elevator door. He's quiet as we ascend.

The doors open and we are behind Mrs. Blake's desk in the reception area. She turns here large body and smiles at both of us. "Mister Caldwell. Miss Davis," she acknowledges. I feel relief sweep through me. She doesn't know.

I see the start of surprise on Mrs. Porto's face as we enter her office. Her eyes narrow at the sight of me and I hesitate for the briefest of seconds. Such dislike is hard to mask and her look frightens me. Mister Caldwell ignores it and leads me into his office. I pull back instinctively when he heads for the black room. He stops and cocks a brow at me. I feel my belly twist.

"Please," I whisper.

"Tell me."

I stammer then swallow quickly. "It frightens me."

He's looking at me curiously. I see the thoughtful glint in his eye and panic builds inside of me. He pulls me forward and opens the door. I'm pushed inside and become disoriented immediately. A different couch is against the wall. No it's the same one with one of the bolsters removed. The spot light shines directly on it.

I can't make out anything else in the room. The light blinds my eyes. Fingers unbutton the coat. It's removed. I shiver and try to shade my eyes. My wrist burns with the smack that hits it. I let it fall. My wrists are clipped tightly together and then I'm pushed backwards, falling, a gasp all that escapes before I land on the soft fur spread out on the couch. My arms are bent and pulled back and attached to each side of the bolster. Shoes are pulled off, stockings slid down. My head is raised and then a thin strap entraps my tongue down in my mouth. I can't see him. I'm blinded by the light.

His voice seems to be disembodied. It reaches me from somewhere above and in front of me. "You have no idea how nice you look all stretched out like that Miss Julia. Black and white are my favorite colors. I love the contrast. Such a soft white body against a soft black background."

A flash of white seems to flicker. I hear a click and then another flash and lick. He's taking pictures. My stomach turns and sickens. "Open your legs."

I can't. I close them tighter. I hear a sigh. My hands are simultaneously released and I'm flipped over and reattached. My belly twists when I hear the cabinet door open. "You're right Miss Julia," he whispers. "A touch of red might be the most interesting."

The riding crop hisses through the air and lands with a sickening crack. I jerk and scream through the gag. The pain bites deep and I have no respite from the blows he gives me. I can barely suck in enough air. A fog seems to invade my brain. All before me is black on black. I don't hear his words when he speaks and the crop comes down heavily. I force myself to concentrate.

"Up on your knees Miss Julia. Stick that ass out." I struggle up onto my knees, my legs shaky and slipping on the soft fur. I hear the click and another. "Spread your legs." I do. Anything not to feel the bite of the crop again. "Tighten your ass." I do. Anything.

I'm turned and positioned again and again. The camera clicks away. I'm beside myself with shame and humiliation. My legs are pulled tightly to each side and attached. I lay stretched and spraddled out like a wanton whore. The camera clicks. My ass pulsates. He brushes my nipple with a finger. I squint against the light but see nothing but a dark shape hovering above me. I desperately need to swallow. "I'll let you stay this way and think over your actions."

He opens the door to his office and then switches off the light leaving me in complete blackness. I don't think he hears my muted scream of terror.

I'm terrified of the dark. I always have been since I was very young and a cousin shut me in a closet in his basement and left me there for a long time. It took my parents days to calm me down after they finally found me. I never liked the dark after that. Even blindfolded, I know there's light. This is nothingness. A void. A chasm that can swallow and devour.

My heart is racing out of control. Sweat beads on my body. I struggle to swallow. Tears leak from my eyes and I sniff hard so I can breathe better. I'm shaking from head to toe. Something brushes my body lightly and my mind leaps with terror. I'm back in the closet, a terrified four year old. Every ghost and goblin I knew of is in there with me. They touch me and stroke me with light feathery fingers. They seem to breathe in my ear and laugh at me from all sides. The dark is a living thing. It pulsates and grows. It's slowly enveloping me and smothering me. I can't breath. I struggle but my throat is paralyzed. I can feel my mind starting to spin with dizziness. I pull in a ragged breath and then another and then I'm screaming out of control.

My cheek explodes with pain and the shock stuns me into silence. I'm never hit in the face. The light is blinding me and I close my eyes against it, struggling against my bonds. I begin to shake and I hear whimpering, unaware it is mine till the gag is released. I swallow and swallow, working my throat. I can't take in an even breath. I start to cry and can't stop. My arms and legs are released and I curl into a ball, hugging myself as I shake and sob.

I'm afraid to open my eyes. I'm terrified I might be back in the darkness. Mister Caldwell hasn't made a sound. I'm not even sure if he's there. Maybe it wasn't him who released me. Maybe it was them.

I jerk violently at the touch on my arm. I hug myself tighter and squeeze my eyes shut. "Miss Julia." The voice wafts over me but it might be a demon pretending. I whimper and bury my head tighter into my drawn up knees. My teeth make a steady chattering sound.

Fingers are grabbing at me and I panic. My arms flail and I kick and scream at the unknown molester. I feel the soft fur under me as I'm raised into the air. My breath leaves in a rush as I'm held tight to a hard body and then I'm in the light of his office. I can't stop shaking and hardly dare to look but a glance upwards shows me two intense dark eyes watching me searchingly. He walks to the couch and sits in the vee of the corner, cradling me tight against his body. I can't stop shaking.

Hands soothe my hot cheek, stroke my hair back from my face, lightly caress my arm. I can't stop shaking. I burrow into his body. I need to feel him. I have to be sure it's him.

"Tell me Miss Julia." His voice is so low. So calm.

I try but my chin trembles violently and I bite my tongue instead. I snap my mouth shut and try again but all that comes out are gasping sobs. I reach up and touch his face lightly. It is him. Relief flows through me so strongly it unnerves me and I weep unrestrainedly. I can do nothing but hold tight to him and bury my face in his neck as the horror of the demons slowly fades. It is the first time I have no thought of his reactions. I don't care what he does to me as long as I can have this minute of comfort.

I lose energy to continue quickly and I end up exhausted and spent. His hand soothes my arm. I'm warm and safe in the confines of fur and his arms. I try to take a deep breath but it wobbles in my throat and ends up as a half yawn. I can feel myself drifting off.

"You're becoming too involved with her." The voice reaches me as if from a long distance and I try to ignore it and drift back to sleep.

"She pleases me." His low voice rumbles silkily beneath my ear.

"She owes me."

"I paid your debt. She was punished."

"I think. . . ."

"You forget your place Mrs. Porto. Return to your work."

"Yes but . . ."

"If you value your job get out."

"But Mister Caldwell I think. . . ."

"I think you've gone too far."

I drift off in the silence that follows. The last thing I hear is his deep sigh.

For the first few days afterwards I am nervous he will use the knowledge of my deep fear to punish me with it. I walk on egg shells and do all I am supposed to. Even Mr. Su has a hard time finding a reason to use his cane.

My body is tight and trimmer than ever before. I work out for an hour and a half every other day with Mr. Su. The opposite days I use the machines under Lars' guidance. I swim in the pool with Lars every day and my muscles are pampered by his strong hands as he massages all the tension and weariness from them each day.

I have the freedom of the apartment except for Mister Caldwell's room. I still haven't seen it. The only times I'm bound to anything is at night or when Lars must leave the apartment. And of course whenever Mister Caldwell wishes it for his own pleasure.

We're eating our dinner in the dining room as usual and I can't keep still. I try hard, seeing the curious looks Mister Caldwell is giving me. I'm on tenterhooks. It is such an important dinner to me.

"Sit still," he hisses and I do. Immediately.

"I'm sorry." I see his scowl and quickly lower my eyes and concentrate on my own meal. I can't seem to swallow anything. I sip my wine and ask for more. I see the surprised lift of his brow and realize I don't care for this kind. I can feel the blush suffuse my face.

Lars comes in to clear the dishes and I hold my breath. Mister Caldwell wipes his mouth and pushes his chair back slightly.

"You have outdone yourself Lars. That was an excellent meal." Happiness surges through me and I feel giddy with relief.

"Miss Julia made it Mister Caldwell."

Surprised eyes turn to me and I feel my heart start to pound. I can't keep the happy smile from my lips. His eyes are assessing and I feel some of my confidence slip.

"You are always a surprise Miss Julia." I can't tell from his tone if he's pleased or not and my smile slowly fades. He said Lars could teach me, I think in sudden alarm as I lower my eyes. I can feel my face paling. I bite my lower lip. I hate his silences.

"Come to me Miss Julia." His voice is low as always. Soft. It suddenly seems menacing.

I rise on shaky legs and walk to him. He turns in his seat and our knees touch. Hand on my waist. Finger lifting my chin. Dark intense eyes searching mine. His sudden wonderful smile throwing me off balance as it always does. "I hope you will make me this meal again. It was delicious."

I feel the happy tears prick at my lids and bite my lip to try to control them. I nod, a small happy laugh of relief escaping before I can stop it. My world is once more light and even. He liked my meal.

He stands and takes my hand. We go into the living room and he pours us each a cordial. "Do you notice anything new?"

I look around and begin to shake my head when my eyes find what he means. There is a picture of me on the opposite wall of the couch. It is large, at least four feet squarer. I am laying down on the black mink, slightly on one hip. One hand covers my mound, the other my breast, though the nipple peeks through the splayed fingers. The other breast lies partially covered beneath the arm. My head is turned and my hair falls partially over my face. The merest hint of the pink welts that are starting to rise show against the whiteness of my backside. My skin is flawless and too white against the black fur.

It is an intriguing picture. It is an arousing picture. It is so obviously me but only to Lars and Mister Caldwell and myself. My tossed hair just covers enough of my face to make it uncertain for everyone else. I never knew anyone who had the courage to ask though I found almost everyone glancing speculatively from it to me many times through the years. It took me a very long time to meet those gazes calmly.

"Do you like it?"

"I'm not sure," I answer honestly. I daren't lie. He's never tolerated it. I'm torn between being proud of my body and the feeling of embarrassment knowing it is on such prominent display. I suddenly wonder what he did with the other pictures he took.

His finger brushes my cheek lightly. "They're only for my pleasure," he murmurs, reading my mind once again. I flush and hear his low chuckle. "Such a delight," he whispers and leads me to the couch.

I stand looking out the windows in the living room. Life goes on in the gray world far below me while I live in a quiet sameness. I like my samensss. I fear the outside world. I've only been out in it twice in the last. . . . . how long?

I don't know. I turn and seek out a newspaper. I don't see them often. Mister Caldwell must read his at the office. I can't locate one and wander into the kitchen. Lars is fussing with dinner. I am always amazed at how dexterous he is for his size. Nothing seems beyond his abilities. Or is it just that my world is so structured and narrow? Little varies from day to day. Just the food we eat, the music Mr. Su plays and the things Mister Caldwell expects me to accept and do.

I see a paper on top of the bag of recycling that Lars collects. The environment is very important to him. I lift it and stop still. The headline is big. A picture of Steve Cochran stares back at me. I'm instantly back in the spare room. My sphincter contracts automatically and I quickly shake myself out of it. The words finally penetrate and I gasp. The former president and his long time pal, the former vice-president, have been killed in a mysterious one car accident. No witnesses. No ideas of how it happened.

The paper is taken from my numb fingers and I stare at Lars in shock. "This has nothing to do with you Miss Julia," he says, his eyes sliding to my right breast. I see the merest hint of his lips tightening and I shudder. It can't be. It's absurd.

Hands turn me and give me a push towards the door of the kitchen. "Go and put on what's on your bed. Mister Caldwell is taking you out after lunch."

The word snap me out of my thoughts and I feel my face pale. "What?" Is that my voice? It sounds so harsh.

"You heard me. Go and do what you're told." His dim eyes are steady and slightly challenging and I turn quickly and obey. I can't seem to separate my thoughts. Mister Caldwell. Out. Steve Cochran. Dead. Lars eyes on my breast. Stop it. Stop it! I cry silently and enter my room.

I can't believe the clothes on the bed. I just stand and stare. A white blouse, long sleeved and high necked. An A-line skirt of thick wool in a muted plaid of lavender and pink. Thick knee high socks. Tall soft black leather boots with low heels and a pale pink cashmere cardigan. The black mink coat is on the back of the chair. The mink hat and pair of fur lined black leather gloves sit on top of it.

I haven't seen this many clothes in months and months. I stand there without moving, not quite able to believe I am supposed to put all these clothes on. I wear thin shifts and go barefoot or corsets and high heels. I don't wear clothes. The one white dress in my closet is sheer and flowing, not heavy like these. I take a step back and walk into Mister Caldwell. His hands take my arms when I jump and try to step away. "Tell me."

I'm still looking at the clothes. I can't see his expression behind me or tell his mood from his voice. I try not to stammer. "I don't know. I think it makes me feel weighed down."

"Well they are necessary. It is bitter cold out and snowing."

I turn in his arms, my eyes startled. "Snowing?"

He watches me steadily. A finger strokes my cheek and he nods. "It just started." Hands on my neck, a thumb tilting my lips upward. His warm exciting lips on mine. Everything shifts as his fingers stroke and caress my nipples. His tongue moves and explores my mouth. My neck. My ear. My breath is fast and shallow. I raise tentative arms to put around his neck but he stops them and clips my wrists behind me. He pulls them into the small of my back and I arch slightly. His lips tease and suck the nipple through the thin material of my shift. I moan and whimper with desire.

I'm pushed gently onto my back on top of the clothes on the bed and then his mouth is between my legs and I'm panting with need as the heat sears into my loins. His expert tongue takes me there quickly and then he fills me and takes me to the brink time and again before letting my insides explode in time with his own. I lay there limp, wanting to put my arms around him so badly but he makes no move to undo my wrists. I feel his breath on my breasts. The lightest kiss on each nipple and then he rises, bringing me with him. We shower but still he doesn't unclip my hands. He tears the shift from me when I am beneath the spray and then he takes his time teasing and tormenting me till I wish to scream with frustration. He kneels before me and sucks my clit into his mouth, his teeth chewing so delicately I orgasm instantly. I feel his hands on my shoulders and sink to my knees but I'm too weak and rest my head on his thigh. i'm raised turned and pushed against the warm wet glass. The sting of the wet washcloth gives me energy and I suck heartily when I kneel before him again. The last thing I have strength for is to cope with having to go out into the world today. As always I have no choice in the matter.

I don't like so many clothes on me. I'm not used to it and I feel like they're choking me. I keep pulling the collar away from my neck during lunch till Mister Caldwell loses patience and attaches my left wrist to the chair. "Eat," he orders putting the fork into my right hand. I try but have trouble swallowing. His glowering stare doesn't help and soon I can't swallow at all without gagging and choking.

I hear his annoyed sigh and swallow the food in my mouth quickly. I choke and cough, trying hard to suck in air. His hand pounds my back and finally I can breathe decently. Tears pour down my cheeks and I blanch at his scowl. "I'm sorry," I whisper, starting to cough all over again.

"You'll have to go hungry," he mutters, releasing my wrist and raising me from the chair. His hand is unusually tight on my arm and I wince in pain. He ignores it. I'm helped into the coat and the hat and he tells me to put on the gloves. I'm starting to shake. I don't want to go. I flinch when the doors open and he pulls me into the elevator. I make a grab for his arm and he allows me to cling to his coat sleeve. I hug his arm tight to my breasts. I don't want to look when the doors open.

I keep my cheek against his shoulder as we walk toward the door. It's the first time I hold onto him instead of him holding tight to me. The air is indeed bitter cold and it takes my breath away. The snowflakes seem to sear my skin and I bury my head into the crook of his elbow. Were they always this cold? I'm oblivious to the muffled up people scurrying by on their own quest to reach warmth. I don't hear the cars or their horns. I just want to reach the car.

I bend and let go of Mister Caldwell's arm when I feel Sam's hand on my elbow. The interior is warm and dim and I again feel safe. I sit and watch the specks of white dissolve into wet spots on the black fur. My hands are clasped tight in my lap. I shiver and snuggle deeper into my coat. The clothes are finally welcomed, not resented. He knows what is best for me. He takes good care of me.

I stare out the window but nothing is familiar to me. I never had had time to learn about the city. My life here has always consisted of the office, my room and his apartment. I know how to get from my old room to the office. I don't even know where his apartment is.

We travel for a long time. The snow gets deeper, the cars and buildings fewer. Mister Caldwell is engrossed in his paperwork and I remain quiet. I watch mountains in the distance. They look so stark. So alone somehow. Their hillsides are bare now but for a few interspersed pines. It makes me sad to think animals of all sorts are trying to survive a cold winter on just what that forbidding mountain will provide for them. Sort of like me. I survive on what Mister Caldwell supplies. He can be as cold and forbidding as the mountain appears to be. Can the mountain ever be warm and loving as he is sometimes?

A touch on my hand rouses me from my thoughts. Mister Caldwell has put his papers away and is watching me steadily. "Tell me why you look so sad?"

"I was just thinking how cold and alone the mountains look."

"The mountain is never alone. It is stately and powerful. Thousands, possibly tens of thousands of creatures from the smallest insect to the largest bird and mammal depend on it. Live on it. Are controlled by its moods.'' His eyes stare at it unflinchingly as his fingers stroke my thigh.

He seems to be far away in his thoughts but his hand travels up my back and I bend to the slight pressure. I release his penis and take it in my mouth. Sucking and licking it into the best it can become as he drives me to distraction with his fingers on my nipples and breasts. I hear his sigh and then he lifts me and I am straddled over his lap, the skirt rucked up and I slide onto his shaft. He lays his head back and directs my movements with just the tip of his fingers on my ass. I desperately want to feel his mouth on my breasts but he never lifts his head. My movements become faster. I grind against him harder. I'm almost in tears with frustration and then his mouth sucks a nipple into it through the fabric of the blouse and he sucks and sucks and I'm coming and coming. I hear his low grunt and then collapse against him, his member still pulsing inside me, the feeling almost tickling in a sexy kind of way. I love laying against his strong body. The moment never lasts long enough for me.

His hands urge me up and he hands me a damp cloth. I wash him and then myself. I'm pulling my skirt back over my legs when I catch Sam's grin in the rearview mirror. I can feel the blood rushing to my face. I hear Mister Caldwell's soft chuckle and feel his finger stroke my hot cheek. ''So delightful,'' he murmurs and then pulls me tight against him with his arm around my shoulder. I'm content to lean against him and watch the changing landscape in silence.

We pull off the narrow road we've been traveling on and turn into an even narrower one. The pine trees seem to close in and form a tunnel that we travel through. I begin to feel a bit uneasy. His face is unreadable. Is he tired of me?

The unbidden thought makes me pale and I feel my face go numb. Would he kill me and bury me out here in the middle of nowhere? As always he seems to know my thoughts. A gentle finger turns my chin. I can't quite keep it from trembling.

"Tell me."

Tears fill my eyes and I bite my lip to try to gain control. "Are you leaving me here?" My voice is more of a squeak than a voice as I blurt out my fears. I see the small smile lift his lips, his expression calm, almost amused.

"And why would I do that?" he asks quietly and I instantly feel foolish and young. I shake my head, my face flaming and feel soft lips lick away my tears. I draw a big breath and hold it for a moment before letting it out slowly. "I'm sorry."

"This is a surprise I think you will like," he says and smiles when my eyes light up with anticipation.

"We're almost there Mister Caldwell," Sam's voice reaches us from the front. I watch Mister Caldwell remove a tube from a side compartment and then he motions me to face him. A very thin layer of grease is spread over my face. "I don't want your skin chapped," he answers my unspoken question. He puts another coat on and then tosses the tube back into the compartment. He reaches into another compartment and pulls out a pair of thick knee length bloomers. I can think of no other word for them. He watches my face and I hear him laugh for the first time. It's a short deep laugh. Actually more of a chuckle but heartier.

"You'll need these in the cold. Can't have your cunt freezing up Miss Julia." His voice is really jovial and I find myself staring at him in surprise. I take the garment at his urging and stare at it a moment longer. The car stopping reminds me to hurry and I pull the pants over my boots. I haven't had anything like pants on in so long, even the soft wool seems scratchy and coarse against my mound. I grimace and once again hear his chuckle.

The door opens and he leaves, his hand reappears a moment later and I step from the car. I'm in a world of white and green and brown. I look up and the sky is an electric blue. So clear. So bright. So big. I stare around as if dumbfounded.

Pine tree after pine tree, from the smallest to the largest, surrounds us. I look questioningly at Mister Caldwell and see his brows arch quizzically. "What do you think."

"I don't know. Why are we here?" I ask before thinking.

"I want you to select our Christmas tree."

He couldn't have uttered any words that would have surprised me more. I gape at him. I can't move. I can't believe I heard the right words. His eyes are steady and I know I heard right. "Me?" I squeak.

He nods and I tear my eyes from him and look all around me. It's too much. I haven't made a decision in so long. This is simple but devastating at the same time. Tree after tree looms in my sight. I don't know. I don't want the responsibility. I shake my head in confusion. It's too much. I can't.

I hear the trunk slam and turn. Mister Caldwell has changed his overcoat for a thick lumberman's type jacket. His head is bare, his hands encased in heavy gloves. I realize he is wearing jeans for the first time. I've never seen him dressed like this. He looks so much younger. He reaches down and picks up an ax that is leaning against the car bumper. His brows lift and he motions me forward.

I walk as if in a trance. I see my breath crystallize in front of me with each exhale I make. One foot goes in front of the other. I can feel the cold slightly through the boots. I pull my hat lower when my ears start to sting. I'm staring at the ground, watching where I place my feet.

"You can't see the trees looking at the ground Miss Julia." His voice is directly behind me and I jump slightly. I nod and look up. Tree after tree meets my gaze. How can one decide on one over another? My mind begins to grapple with the task he's set me. "How tall can it be?"

"Twelve feet."

Two of him, I think. I look at him and try to imagine him standing on his own shoulders. Twelve feet. My eyes search the trees but I don't see anything about that height. I move forward, suddenly excited about making the decision. I move from one glade to another, always checking to be sure he's with me and then I see it. It is the most perfect tree I have ever seen. Perfectly proportioned. The perfect height. A glorious deep green.

I turn excited eyes to his and see his nod of agreement, the smile wide on his face. I'm almost bursting with pride. I've done it. I've found a good tree. He likes my choice.

I watch in wonder as he motions me away and then lifts the ax and begins to fell the tree. The ax strikes and the sound is sharp and poignant in the cold silent air. A few moments later Sam is beside me, rope in hand. I feel my belly twist lightly. My feet begin to shuffle nervously as my mind wonders what he has in store for me.

"Timber." Mister Caldwell's voice rings out and then the woods are full of the sound of the tree crashing to the ground. Sam moves towards it and hands Mister Caldwell one end of the rope. I watch in relief as they use it to tie the tree tightly. Sam drags it towards the car and then we're alone again.

I no longer have a purpose and stand there unsure of what to do. I see him looking at me, his breath is rapid, the color in his cheeks high. A slow smile spreads his lips and the next thing I know he bends and then I'm hit with a snowball directly on my chest. I stare down at the snow and don't know how to react.

My hand lifts to wipe it off. I raise my eyes to his. He's still grinning. Do I dare retaliate? Is it allowed? My heart is pounding with indecision. I dread doing anything to spoil the day. "Afraid you'll miss," he taunts me in a whisper and then my face is wet as a loose snowball hits it gently.

It breaks my uncertainty. I reach down and form a snowball, pelted with two more before I can lift it. I toss it towards him but he dodges it easily. Time shifts and I'm home in my backyard with my father. He's throwing ball after ball at me and I'm returning them just as quickly. I duck behind a tree for cover and make a hurried pile. I see the red of a jacket and throw one, laughing aloud when I see it strike the arm. The figure comes nearer and I shriek in delighted fright and scoop up a few snowballs before I run, seeking shelter. My head is hit, my hat goes flying. I turn and throw mine, delighted when I see one hit his face. I see the surprise but then the face fades and shifts and it's no longer my father's. I stay still in sad surprise and then I'm tackled and hit the snow lightly, a body following me down immediately.

I feel his fast breath hitting my face. It feels warm in the cold air. His eyes are alight with merriment and I melt under the wide smile. Lips touch mine and then the kiss deepens and things shift again. I feel my skirt lifted, the tingle of gooseflesh crawl up my body as the cold penetrates to the skin. I hear his soft curse when he encounters the underwear. The seams give and then he's easing into me, the feeling of fullness welcomed. I move under him. I feel the soft fur under my bare backside, the hardness of him inside me. His tongue probes and searches my mouth. Kisses follow along my jaw, my ear, my neck. Everything is in contrast. Warm kisses are followed by icy coldness. Fullness is followed by emptiness as he moves in and out of me. The need flows and builds. I want more of him. I want to feel his skin on mine. I want to feel his mouth all over my body. I want him. I have him. I come with him. I cry. And I don't know why.

We sip hot chocolate from a thermos on the way home. I snuggle deep into the crook of his arm and think back over the day. Again something seems to have changed but I can't put my finger on it. The relationship has shifted somehow but how I don't know.

"When is Christmas?" I ask quietly. I hold my breath wondering if he'll answer me. I'm surprised when he does.

"Today is Thanksgiving. It's four weeks till Christmas."

Thanksgiving. It's already the end of November. I've been with him since May. Five months. It doesn't seem possible. I'm quiet for the rest of the ride home.

The tree is set up in the far corner of the living room. Lars moves it effortlessly around until Mister Caldwell feels it's in the best position. We three dine together on Lars' fabulous Thanksgiving feast and then Mister Caldwell and I sit in the living room staring at the tree for a while. He leaves me loose and reads to me. It is the first time I have spent the entire day with my hands free. I wonder if he'll leave me free for the night. He doesn't.

Mr. Su is in a particularly foul mood when I enter the room and I suffer frequently under his cane. He seems to be seeking a reason. His hands rove too freely but I make no move to stop him. I've been told to obey him and I do. No one has ever asked me if he touches me. No one has ever commented on the red marks on my body after I finish a session with him.

I'm on my hands and knees, trying to stretch my leg to the side as he's instructing. He turns up the music and comes up behind me and kneels. I can feel the bulge in his pants and I tighten up. He grabs my right leg and holds it out straight to the side. I pant with pain, the muscles stretching cruelly. He's rubbing himself against my backside. I swallow and stay still. My stomach is turning. I feel the tube seeking the crease of my backside, rubbing itself into it for more friction. He stops, my leg lowers slightly and then he pushes his released penis between my legs and pushes my legs together tight with his own. He humps and pumps, his fingers holding cruelly to my waist. I feel his nails, I hear his ragged breath and something snaps and I pull forward and collapse. I hear his yell of rage at the same time I feel the sticky semen hit my thighs. The sharp pains follow immediately and I try to crawl away. I know he is beyond anger and I'm truly afraid of him for the first time. I feel my head clasped between two legs and I'm held helpless as blow after blow lands on my bare behind. I claw at his legs, my screams strangled in my throat by the tight hold he maintains on my neck. I feel a wetness on my rear and then I pass out.

I wake up in my bed. Lars is soothing salve over the tops of my thighs and backside. It throbs and pulses and I begin to cry. Mister Caldwell's beatings never hurt like this. This is purer pain. Nothing but intense pain. I try hard to stammer out an explanation but most of my words are incoherent, even to myself.

I'm in terror of Mister Caldwell's reactions but then the large fingers are gone and smaller, strong hands are pulling my upper body onto his lap. He strokes and soothes my cheek, brushing the hair from my tear stained face. "It's all right," he whispers from above me and I feel something give inside of me. I grab his legs and hold on for dear life as I cry till I can't anymore.

My crying eases as I lose strength and I doze off on his lap, waking guiltily a short while later. I lift my head and look upward but he is leaning back against the headboard, his one hand on my back the other arm over his eyes as his head rests against the wall. I don't know what to do. Is he asleep. Thinking? I lay my head back down and again doze, finding myself alone next when I wake.

I see the two cuts where he drew blood the next morning. Mister Caldwell has never drawn blood. I can't help but wonder if it's over with yet. Will I be punished for fighting him? I grimace with pain as I move. I hope the punishment won't be working out with Mr. Su tomorrow. I don't know if I could stand it. I don't know if I could do it.

Nothing is said and I don't see Mr. Su till the following week. I walk into the room with Lars and stop in my tracks. Mr. Su is waiting for us. His right shoulder and right arm are encased in a cast. Lars sits in a chair in the corner of the room and I begin my lesson. Mr. Su stays in one place and directs me only with his voice. A very shaky voice. His eyes constantly flick to Lars in the corner. I don't see him but once more and then am instructed to follow a video every other day. It chills me to the bone to see the unconcern. I can only assume Lars paid him a visit. I can't work up the courage to ask either one and nothing in way of an explanation is offered.

This is the second person that has hurt me and ended up hurt. Is there a connection? What about M. Lafouche? Or his son? I have no way to find out. I wouldn't get an answer if I ever did work up the courage to ask. I try to block it from my mind. It constantly creeps in at night. I find I'm both flattered and appalled if it is true.

We decorate the tree the following week and I'm thrilled when Mister Caldwell helps and admires the tree over and over. When he takes me to my room that night I finally work up the courage to ask what I've been wanting to for the past two weeks.

"Mister Caldwell do you have my money I had saved?" I see the surprise and hastily go on. "I was hoping you would let me have some of it so I could buy Lars a Christmas gift. I mean I was hoping you would do it for me," I quickly amend, seeing the suspicion enter his eyes. He watches me steadily and I feel the flush creep up my cheeks. I can't meet his eyes. "I'm sorry," I whisper.

Hands turn me around and I'm pushed onto my stomach on the bed. My shift is lifted and I grab onto the blanket waiting for the pain. He lets me wait. I bury my head in the crook of my arm. I hate the waiting. I never should have asked. Hands stroke my cheeks, the marks of Mr. Su are faded and gone. Fingers find and manipulate my clit. I try hard not to clench my legs. Lips brush my rear and I tense as they make their way lower. A tongue flicks out and laves my vulva. I feel my legs shaking with need. Fingers, tongue, fingers, tongue. I'll lose my mind someday from this wonderful torture he puts me through daily. I feel the heat intensify, the touch of a tongue on my anus making me jerk in lewd surprise. The knob is like ivory, smooth and hard and then he pushes all the way in. I gasp at the pain but it lessens immediately.

He lays over me, his breath tickling my ear, his tongue licking the lobe. "Tense your bottom Miss Julia." His words are soft, hushed and I obey. I flex and loosen my sphincter around his shaft. I hear his sigh of pleasure and try harder to please him. His fingers seek my bud, his tongue teases my ear and I'm over the edge. He pumps me hard as my body still spasms, his low grunt reaching my ears a short moment later. He lays over me for a long time, his penis slowly easing from me as it shrinks.

I find my five hundred and thirty four dollars on the night table the next morning after Lars releases me. Mister Caldwell has left early for the office and I follow Lars around all morning, trying to find out what he might want without arousing his suspicions. He lets me help him with dinner after our swim and then I work up the courage to ask what I've wanted to all day.

"Lars would you buy a gift for me for Mister Caldwell?"

The dim eyes swivel towards me and watch me steadily. Did he learn that from his boss? It unnerves me but I force myself to go on. "He's given me my money that I had and I want so much to buy him a soft cashmere pullover. I can't do it but I thought maybe you would for me." The eyes don't even blink and I find myself losing courage. "I'm sorry," I whisper, feeling guilty but having no idea why. Both of them can make me feel this way so easily. I turn away and keep tearing the lettuce, aware of the eyes boring into my back. I'm near tears and fighting them. Lars has only smacked me the one time and I suddenly wonder if he's going to do it again. I feel myself tightening in anticipation of the pain.

"I wouldn't know what color," he mumbles a minute later and I turn surprised eyes back to him. His smile is such a rare thing it always makes me respond with one of my own.

"I could look through magazines if you'd bring me some and find a color you could try to match," I suggest breathlessly, excited that I'll be able to give Mister Caldwell a gift on Christmas morning. I love the feel of cashmere against my cheek when he wears one of his and lets me lie next to him on the couch. I have a picture in my mind of what he'll look like in a shirt of soft yellow. It will go well with his brown curly hair. All I have to do is figure out what to buy Lars.

The coffee table is full of fashion magazines and catalogs the next morning and I spend hours looking through them. None are exactly what I want but I finally settle for something close to what I had in mind. I show Lars, watch him hitch up his pants as he studies the picture thoughtfully and notice the tear in his leather belt. Two problems settled at once.

I'm antsy during dinner and can barely sit still. I see his scowl and try harder. Lars is in and out of the room so I can't broach the subject till we retire to the living room. I watch him pour himself a brandy, pause and then pour another. I'm surprised. He's never offered me brandy before. He hands it to me and then turns on the stereo. Strauss fills the air. He turns once more and clinks my glass in a silent toast. I breathe deeply, a smile on my lips. I love these special moments.

We sit side by side on the couch and he leans his head on the back of the seat. His arm is around my shoulder and his hand plays with my breast in a negligent fashion. His eyes close and again I wait impatiently, barely able to keep from squirming under the teasing touch of his hand. I sip the brandy. I don't like it.

I hold the glass in my hands on my lap. I wait. His hand stops moving and I wonder if he's dozed off. I watch the hand on his leg holding the glass. I see no slackening. I shift slightly and he lifts his head. He takes a sip, sees my glass and raises his brows.

"Drink your brandy Miss Julia."

I do. I can't help the small shudder that ripples along my spine. I see his amused smile and grow courageous.

"Mister Caldwell would you buy Lars a new belt for me to give him at Christmas?" His lips purse and I hurry on. "I saw his is ripped and I can give you the money now." My face crimsons as I realize how foolish the last words are when he smiles at me with amusement. He'd given me my money. He knew I had it. "You'll have to tell me how much you'll need," I murmur. Fingers lift my chin and soft lips caress mine. I open my mouth automatically and feel the gentle swipe of his tongue on mine.

"I have to go to Spain on business for a week anyway. I'll buy it there. They have excellent leather goods."

His words stun me and I feel instant panic. My eyes fly to his and I beg silently for him not to leave me. I see his small smile, feel the gentle finger stroke my neck. "No my pet. You are not ready to travel with me yet."

"I'll be good. I'll obey you," I whisper desperately.

His laugh is amused and low. "You obey me because you must. No," he says with a sigh. "The time is not right. One day you will accompany me. You still have much to learn." I know the conversation is over but I feel I must try again. "Lars could. . . . ."

"No." The word is hard and clipped and I stop, defeated. I feel weighed down and sadder than I have for a long time. I can't shake a small feeling of panic that lingers. I am afraid of his being gone. He's always here. I miss him terribly already. No being held. No being stroked. No Mister Caldwell.

I can't shake the depression that engulfs me and he becomes annoyed. I try to listen to him but my mind keeps sliding to what I imagine a week without him will be like. Twice I've not heard his questions and I see the hardening of his lips. "I'm sorry," I apologize but he yanks me to my feet and pulls me to my room. The shift is ripped off, I'm attached low in the shower and he buggers me viciously. He leaves me there and doesn't return for a while. I'm released and kneel before him, hands tight behind me as I take him in my mouth. He makes me go on and on before finally unloading in my mouth. My mouth aches. I'm led into the bedroom and he spread-eagles me face down and ties me tight to the bed. Fingers caress and tease my slit and everything shifts as the feeling grows and builds.

A sharp slap to my rear intensifies the feeling and then his fingers are gone and he's whispering in my ear. "Remember the feeling Miss Julia." I don't hear him leave. I squirm for a long time till the need slowly disappears. He's gone in the morning and so is a hundred dollars from my money.

I am learning how much I need Mister Caldwell. I wander the apartment listlessly. There is no one to look forward to. There will be no touching, no caresses night after night till he decides to return. I even miss his smacks.

Lars is massaging me after my workout and his fingers are doing their wonderful magic. It's been two days of no touching and I yearn for it. His fingers manipulate my buttocks and go to the top of my thighs. I feel the slightest tingling and almost unconsciously try to wiggle down closer to his fingers. I hear the rasp of leather and then the sting of his belt on my backside. I scream in agony and clutch my burning rear with my hands, jumping and writhing on the table as he holds me to it with one hand on the small of my back. I groan and cry, the heat searing my ass. "I'm sorry, I'm sorry," I cry over and over again.

With his incredible strength I'm indeed lucky he only gave me one. I feel its sting all day and I burn with humiliation every time I see Lars. I can't believe I behaved so badly. He never says one word about it. Will he tell Mister Caldwell?

Each night I am attached tightly to the bed face down. I know it's partly punishment, partly so I can't play with myself. I eat a lonely breakfast. Lars insists I finish it and I do but most of it is cold by the time I'm done. My tea is tepid but he makes me finish it as well. I rise to leave but his voice stops me.

"Go and get dressed Miss Julia." I look down and see my shift. I turn puzzled eyes to him but he motions me away towards my room and I go obediently.

Basic black dress, black stockings and garters and black heels are on the bed. The mink coat, hat, black gloves and a small pocketbook lay over the back of the chair. A feeling of fear crawls over me. Mister Caldwell isn't here; he's in Europe. What does this mean? I'm not allowed outside.

Lars enters the room and without a word, disrobes me and starts to dress me. The dress fits snugly and comes to my knees. He brushes my hair but leaves it long. He holds the coat for me and I slip my arms into it. I watch his face as he buttons it but as always it's expressionless. "Lars I don't understand," I whisper but he ignores it.

I notice he isn't wearing jeans and boots but dress pants, loafers, and an open necked shirt. He leads me to the elevator and there dons an enormous black overcoat. It makes him seem even more massive.

The doors open and I hold back, the old fear coursing through me. He pulls me into the elevator without effort and again I make a wild grab for an arm. "I'll be punished," I whisper fearfully. Is this Lars' revenge?

I can't stop shaking and flinch when the doors open. "Lars please," I beg pitiously as he pulls me from the elevator.

He stops and grabs my arms, lifting me so I'm even with his eyes. My feet dangle in mid air. "Stop the nonsense Miss Julia. We're going Christmas shopping for Mister Caldwell's gift."

I see annoyance in his gaze for the first time and nod my head quickly. I feel my feet touch the ground and then Sam is at the glass doors and I'm hit with the cold air and noise. Lars follows me into the car and sits opposite me. He leans forward and stares at me intently. "I want no nonsense from you. This is a treat."

I nod, acknowledging the unspoken threat. I look out the window and watch the endless traffic and people. I can't seem to stop shaking. We pull up outside a huge department store and I watch in growing alarm the amount of people going in and out. I can't go in with that many people. My breathing is too fast. I swallow and cringe back when the door opens but Lars has my arm and is almost dragging me out of the car behind him. A warning squeeze and a glare cease my struggles. "Miss Julia," he growls ominously and I try hard to fight the rising panic. I clutch at his hand on my arm and he shakes it off easily.

I watch the doors growing nearer as he leads me to them and I flinch as they open when we approach. A doorman tips his hat at us and I see him as if from a distance as I'm jostled by the hurrying crowd. I feel the pressure ease on my arm and start to panic. I turn and make a wild grab for Lars but one hard look from him makes me stop. He takes my arm lightly and we start to move through the crowd. Nothing is real. The swarms of people around me seem to close in but then they part before us quickly, Lars' enormous size causeing all to eagerly get out of his way. I can't believe it's real. I seem to be walking in a dream. Everything is slowed down. Everything seems to have a mystical quality as if it is happening somewhere else and I'm watching it as an outsider. I wince under the pressure on my arm and come back to reality abruptly.

A man in a business suit is asking me a question and I try to concentrate. I miss most of what he says and he's giving me a queer look.

"Miss Julia is looking for a cashmere pullover." Lars voice sounds above me and I look up as if in a daze. I see his eyes narrow slightly and feel the slight shake on my arm. I force myself to pay attention.

"What color has Madam in mind?"

"Uh, um a soft yellow I think." My voice sounds strained and I clear my throat. "Yes a soft shade of yellow would be best."

"This way," he says with a small flourish of his hands and I find myself following him. I glance quickly back but Lars is right behind me and I flash him a shaky grateful smile. I see his encouraging nod and start to relax.

I'm led to the rear of the store and after the hustle and bustle of the masses throughout the rest of the store, this seems like a safe quiet haven. The man rummages through a shelf or two and approaches me with a handful of yellow pullovers.

"What size is your husband?"

The word and the question throw me completely. Husband? Size? I'm confused and start to stammer but Lars' hand on my shoulder makes me take a deep breath and think. "I believe he is a large."

I look up and see the agreeing nod from Lars and feel some of the tension ease. I'm shown one style after another and find the simplest of decisions difficult. I don't make decisions. I narrow it down to three and am at sea. Lars leans down and looks them over carefully. "Which one Lars?"

"It's up to you Miss Julia," he murmurs and then sees the panic in my eyes. His own soften almost imperceptively and he smiles. "Which would you like to see Mister Caldwell in?"

I look at the three shirts differently. Only one has a vee neck and I imagine slipping my fingers along the slit and feeling his chest. I smile happily at the thought and lift it confidently. "This one."

"Very good. If Madam will follow me to the register."

I do and as I wait I catch sight of myself in a full length mirror. I see a very sophisticated rich young woman staring back at me and I stare in amazement. Lars catches my eyes in the mirror and smiles and I smile back happily. I suddenly feel much more confident.

"That will be $452.00 Madam." My confidence crumbles and I scrounge hastily in my pocketbook. Where I think the additional eighteen dollars will appear from I don't know. I can feel my hands starting to shake and then Lars holds out a twenty dollar bill to me. I look at it and shake my head, near tears. "I won't be able to pay you back." My voice is on the edge and I try hard to keep my emotions in check.

My purse is taken and the money removed. He hands it to the man who is looking at me strangely and then pockets the change that is given back to him. I feel the pocketbook thrust back into my hands and my arm taken and then we're making our way back to the outside of the building. I get impressions of Christmas decorations and trees but then we're outside in the cold air and waiting at the curb for Sam. A man dressed as Santa approaches us and I lean back into Lars' body. He removes the two loose dollars from his pocket and puts it into my stiff fingers. I look at it stupidly and then see the Santa's hand raised to take it. I give it to him, a stiff smile on my face and then the car rounds the corner and Sam's opening the door and Lars is handing me inside and I finally give into the shakes I've been fighting all this time.

I sit clutching my pocketbook tight to my chest, trying desperately to stop hyperventilating. Lars' hand pats my knee gently. "You did fine Miss Julia," he praises me but all I can do is give him a shaky smile. I want Mister Caldwell. I need to be held. I wish I could ask

Lars to hold me if only for a moment but the memory of his huge hand on my rear dries up the words before they can be uttered. He takes care of me but shows no affection for me. Maybe it's the only way he can do it, I wonder briefly.

I remember I have no wrapping paper when we return to the apartment but Lars assures me he'll pick some up when he goes out tomorrow. "Can I come with you?"

"No."

I search for someplace to hide the gift but my room is too open. There is no place Mister Caldwell might not look. I ask Lars if he'll keep it in his room and he reluctantly agrees.

I'm staring out the living room windows when Lars calls me back to my room. "I have to go out Miss Julia. Go to the bathroom."

I do as he says and then stretch out face down on the bed. He attaches my arms to the headboard and ties my feet loosely. I resign myself to a few hours of nothing but contemplation.

A short while later I faintly hear the two tones of the intercom. I lay wondering who is calling. It always seems that Lars or Mister Caldwell know when to expect someone. They never seem to be surprised.

My world suddenly goes black as a hood is placed over my eyes. I feel the cords tighten and cut into my cheeks. I gasp in fright and feel the cut of a riding crop across the tops of my thighs. Why? What did I do? When did he come home? I went out with Lars. I start to panic.

My breathing is irregular, my heart is racing. "Mister Caldwell Lars told me to go. I had no choice," I whimper, my head yanked back and I feel a ball gag inserted into my mouth but this has hard pointy spikes on it and it tears the tender lining of my mouth. I moan with pain.

I mew plaintively and receive another cut of the crop. I am writhing against my bonds. These seem so hard, so vicious. I don't understand. It couldn't be Lars could it?

My ankles are let loose and then loops encircle my thighs and they're pulled up and forward so I'm forced onto my knees. I hear the click of clips and feel the pull on the back of my necklace. I'm laying face down with my ass high in the air. My stomach clenches with fear. Why? My ankles are again encircled with loops and they're pulled wide and attached to the foot board. I'm bent as if in supplication. I have no defenses. I have no idea of why he's doing this to me.

The pain hits me unexpectedly. It bites deep into my flesh and digs in deeper. The crop falls again and again and I cannot even move an inch to avoid it without pulling the necklace so tight I start to lose consciousness.

I sense him behind me between my legs and then I scream in agony into the painful gag as the double ridged dildo is forced into me. I thought I couldn't experience any worse pain than I had but this is intolerable. I feel my insides tearing, the blood the only lubrication. I began to choke on the gag, each spasm sending the spikes deeper into my mouth. I strain against the bonds, wishing for the blessed blackness of unconsciousness to take me away from the pain of the remorseless pounding he is giving me. Why? is the last thing I think before I finally succumb to the smothering pressure on my neck.

I wake now and again, images of white on white floating past my eyes and then the blackness covers me again. Pain pulses through me and then a small prick on my backside and oblivion. I open my eyes and see him staring at me from a chair by the wall. I flinch when he rises, a lethargic kind of terror invading my motionless body.

"Why?" I sink back down into nothingness before he can answer.

A man in white is looking down at me searchingly. He's sold me. I start to cry and cannot stop. Another prick of my skin and I know no more.

I open my eyes and a woman is standing by the bed holding my wrist. I try to move but my limbs are heavy. Has he still got me tied down? She smiles at me and I try to speak but drowsiness covers me and I drift off before words can form.

The room is dim, only a small light on the side of my bed. This must be a room I haven't seen. Can it be his I wonder. I remember the man in white. I'm someplace else. I whimper and feel the tears. Why? He looms into my sight and I try to cry out. Soft fingers stroke my cheek, brush the hair from my forehead.

"It wasn't me," he whispers. "It wasn't me." I try to look into his eyes but they are shadowed and dark. His fingers are so gentle. This is the Mister Caldwell I love.

"It wasn't me Miss Julia," he whispers once more and I again fall prey to the overwhelming tiredness that descends on me.

I wake the next morning and find Mister Caldwell, Lars and a man in white staring at me. They all smile down at me and I can't help the happy flutter I feel in my chest. My weak smile trembles and fades. Had I dreamed last night or had he really said it wasn't him? His hand covers mine and I know he's read my thoughts again. "You didn't dream it Miss Julia. It wasn't me."

I can't stop the tears. I'm not even sure why I'm crying. I take a breath and hold it for a long minute and let it out slowly. "I'm sorry," I murmur shakily. His fingers stroke my cheek, my lips and I see a warm, could it be loving, smile on his face I've never seen before. I frown when the man in white intrudes and he lets go of my hand. I see the stethoscope around his neck and everything clicks into place. I'm in a hospital.

"How long have I been here?" I ask trying to see around him as he leans over me and listens to my heart.

"Four days. Lie still." I do. I'm used to taking orders. He straightens and nods his head. "You had us worried for a while. You're not to worry though. You can still have children and will be fine in a few weeks. I want you to give yourself at least six weeks before you have intercourse again. Longer before you have anal intercourse. You were pretty badly torn up inside. Under no circumstances are you to have any sexual activity without an okay from me. Understand?"

I nod, knowing it isn't my decision. Mister Caldwell approaches the bed and assures the doctor he'll make sure of it. The man leaves and I suddenly feel shy and unsure of myself.

"Why?" I can't seem to let go of the question.

"As revenge against me."

I'm totally bewildered and shake my head helplessly. "I don't understand."

"You will in time," he assures me with a pat on my hand. End of conversation.

Lars approaches the other side of the bed and I smile tiredly at the gentle giant. "You almost gave me a heart attack when I found you that way Miss Julia.'' His smile is so tender I feel my eyes filling up again and blink rapidly.

I spend three more days in the hospital. Mister Caldwell or Lars are always in the room with me. I think the nurses were shocked the first time I had to use the bedpan and Lars picked me up and placed me on it without thought. I ignored them and was just happy for the man's strength that made it easier for me. The examinations are painful and for me embarrassing, which makes no sense of all. I see Mister Caldwell's small shake of his head as he smiles his amused smile every time I blush when some intern comes in to check me. Lars is his steady self. He remains pretty much quiet unless someone comes in and I argue with them about something. He won't let them hassle me about eating or washing me but won't let me refuse any medication or examination. I feel like I'm being let out of prison when Mister Caldwell finally comes to collect me.

Sam is at the limousine, holding the door open and smiles broadly at me. ''So glad you feel all right Miss Julia. You gave us quite a scare,'' he says sincerely and again I'm hard pressed to control my tears. Lars sits up front with him and Mister Caldwell cuddles me on his lap all the way home. He kisses my cheek, my eyes, my ear. Tenderly, softly. He strokes my cheek, my neck. Not to arouse, not to torment, but only to comfort. I've missed him so badly.

Mister Caldwell carries me to the elevator and through the apartment. My room is completely changed. The walls are a soft pink and the carpeting is a deep burgundy. The bed is a tall four post tester bed and is piled high with pillows. There is a chaise lounge in one corner and the cabinet is gone.

I turn startled eyes to him but he lays me on the bed

and ignores my questioning look. ''Sleep for a while and then Lars has a surprise for you.'' His lips touch my forehead and he leaves without shutting the door behind him, the thick carpeting as always masking any sound. I lay there, happily tired and let my eyes rove. They have a will of their own and constantly drift to where the cabinet was. Is that part over? Is the relationship changing again?

Lars' surprise is a Jacuzzi whirlpool bath in my bathroom. I'm carried to it and placed into it's swirling jets of water and close my eyes and savor the wonderful feeling. I can't stop smiling and I open my eyes to find both men smiling down at me.

''I take it you approve,'' Mister Caldwell teases and I can do nothing but nod happily.

''It's an early Christmas present,'' Lars mutters. Does he look embarrassed? I can't tell and he hastens off leaving Mister Caldwell standing above me watching me. I feel suddenly self conscious and wish he would join me so he wouldn't tower over me this way. I can't seem to meet his eyes.

A gentle finger strokes my cheek and I look back up. He's watching me with a funny look on his face and I can't decipher it. My heart starts beating madly and I have to swallow quickly. One side of his lip raises in a quirky kind of smile and I relax again.

''My room looks beautiful,'' I murmur.

''I picked the color for the walls by remembering the delightful color of your cheeks when you blush.'' The compliment causes me to do just that and I hear his soft laugh, feel his finger once more. Soft lips touch mine and then I'm alone.

I sink lower into the roiling water and let the water jets and heat do their magic. I'm totally confused but delighted. I'm being pampered, coddled. I love it. Will it all go back to the way it was when he can use me again? Who did this to me? I hate not knowing. I want to know why. If it was revenge against him how did they know I was here and vulnerable? Who knew? Mister Caldwell, maybe. And Lars. I shudder convulsively.

No. It can't have been Lars. Lars' legs would never have fit between my legs to use the dildo. As big and wicked as the apparatus is, it is tiny compared to his own prodigious size. He is much too massive. I would have felt the bed shift. I feel my body starting to shake and force myself to think back.

I remember the slight struggle to bind me tightly. It wasn't someone too strong. I must know them if they kept so silent. I don't know anyone. My head begins to throb and I force myself to relax and let the thoughts go.

The next two weeks are easier. The doctor comes twice a week and checks me. Is this why the cabinet is gone? He says I am doing well. I can walk around now without hardly any discomfort. Mister Caldwell is bathing me again and shaving me in the shower. I almost cry the first time he attaches me. I foolishly thought it was over. That night is the first night I notice the small hooks on the inside of the posts of my bed.

I kneel before him almost every day. He is gentler than before but I'm beginning to wonder if he isn't just biding his time. For a short time after I had first come home from the hospital I had lived in a wonderful fantasy that things were going to be different from now on. As each day passes and we fall more and more back into the old routine, I realize very little is changed. How can I mourn something that never was?

Christmas Eve morning we eat in the kitchen because the dining room table is set for twelve. I can't help being nervous. I don't like when the unexpected occurs. Who is coming? I hear the two tones of the intercom and am hurried into my room. I stand and listen to the soft snick of the lock as the door closes behind him when he leaves. I shiver with apprehension and approach the door. Laying my ear against it does nothing. Silence is all that is heard. I pace. I hate the not knowing. I hate the waiting. He can't be giving me to somebody. I'm not allowed yet.

I doze on my bed and wake to find him naked over me. I see a glint in his eye and it frightens me. His breathing is faster than normal as if he has exerted himself. He pulls me lower on the bed and sits on my chest. He reaches behind him and the shift tears and disappears. I can't take my eyes from him.

"Cup your breasts.

I stare, not understanding and feel his fingers bite into my scalp. "Cup your breasts with your hands."

I do, still at a loss. He lowers his head and licks between the pushed together mounds and then places his penis in the tight valley. "Push them together."

I do and he pumps in and out, the friction of my breasts hugging his tube bringing him off quickly. I find it humiliating for some reason and turn my head, unable to look at him or watch. I feel the sticky spurts hit my neck and chest and then his hand is rubbing it onto my breasts. A fingers flicks my cheek and I look at him. I still don't like his expression. "You still have much to learn Miss Julia," he whispers and then he is gone.

I lay there confused. What had happened when I was locked in my room that had excited him so much? I'm afraid of dinner time. Maybe I won't be a part of it. Maybe I won't attend. I don't want to. I'm told shortly later I will.

He comes to me late in the afternoon. We shower, he shaves me, I suck him. There is an underlying excitement in him and it frightens me. I can feel it by how tense his body is. It unnerves me the speculative way he keeps staring at me.

Stockings, garters, shoes. The same routine but the corset is different. It holds and pushes the breasts upward, exaggerating their fullness and size. My heart is racing. I keep licking my lips as my mouth goes dry. I hate his silence. I hate my lack of courage to ask questions. Why? He wouldn't answer them anyway.

The dress is gold sequins. It is low, extremely low. My breasts bulge dangerously over the neckline. Only the tightness of the bodice keeps my nipples covered. Spaghetti straps and to the floor. A slit up the front, from floor to almost my crotch, is the only thing that allows me to walk and I still cannot take normal steps.

My hair is brushed and twisted into a chignon. A gold comb decorates the side. How does he do it so effortlessly? My make-up is darker than usual. My eyes are more heavily outlined in black. I clasp my hands tightly into my lap to control their shaking.

A finger strokes my cheek and I meet his eyes in the mirror. "My guests have graciously agreed to allow you to see them tonight. You will not have to wear a mask."

I nod. My mouth is bone dry. I try to work saliva

into it but fail. He takes my arm and leads me into the living room. I expect to be attached to the pillar but he seats me on the couch. I sit there and try to keep the skirt from falling to each side of my legs, exposing me.

I hear the click of his tongue. "I went to great expense so the dress would be just as it is. Leave it Miss Julia. Sit with your legs together. It is enticing. Do not cross your legs. It is seductive because one cannot be sure if it is you or shadow they see."

I don't like the tone of warning I hear. I clasp my hands and feel a shiver run up my spine as I hear the two tones. Lars pushes a button and soon after I hear the whoosh of the doors opening.

Two men in white robes step out, look around and then move aside. Two more men follow and I see the look of welcome one gives to Mister Caldwell who has stepped up to greet him. I cannot hear their words. The doors close and a few minutes later they reopen and six men step out. They all look alike. White robes, white headpieces, dark beards, hooked noses, swarthy skins. I see the man talking to Mister Caldwell make introductions and then raise his brows he spies me.

They all approach but four. Bodyguards? "This is Miss Julia."

I nod and automatically lift my hand when he raises his. I see all eyes peer between my legs and then I am on my feet and standing at Mister Caldwell's side. I can not stop the faint blush that touches my cheeks.

Black eyes appraise me from all sides. I want nothing more than to shrink back into Mister Caldwell but do not dare. The man who seems to be in charge narrows his eyes and smiles. I do not like his smile. "She is indeed lovely. Such white skin." His tongue flicks over his lips like a serpent's. I swallow and he grins evilly when I flinch from his outstretched hand. His brows raise. "The little love bird hasn't had her wings clipped?"

"Not completely. She is still being trained."

I wince at the words and again see the evil smile. I hear the low amused laughter of his companions. I can feel my face paling as his hand reaches out once more. It is dark, hairy and perfect manicured. The fingers move along the top mounds of my breast and I cringe. I feel Mister Caldwell's hands on my arms from behind keeping me still. The Arab's smile widens. "I would deem it an honor to be able to teach her obedience. We have methods that never fail. I would return her to you as the perfect slave."

A light kiss on the back of my neck makes me shudder slightly."But half the fun is in the teaching my friend," Mister Caldwell says softly. I watch the knowing smile spread over the dark face before me.

"You are absolutely correct," he acknowledges with a smile and small bow. My arms are released and Mister Caldwell comes to stand beside me. He takes my hand and lifts it to kiss my fingers. The Arab drops his hand from my body.

"Besides, I have both a favor to ask and a gift to give to you. They are really almost one and the same."

Dark brows raise and I hear the hushed murmurings around us cease. "You intrigue me," the dark man says, rubbing his hands in anticipation.

Mister Caldwell smiles and I shiver. I am suddenly terrified. I see the Arab's eyes flick from him to me and I start under the touch of Mister Caldwell's hand on my arm. "Easy." he soothes me in a quiet voice but I can't help but pull back slightly. The pressure of his fingers increases and I suck in my breath sharply. "Come along Miss Julia. I think you should see the gift I have for the Sheik."

He is leading me down the hallway to the spare

rooms. I'm putting one foot in front of the other only because I have no choice. The pressure on my arm is relentless. I seem to have entered the other dimension again. I don't feel my feet. I don't feel my body. Why would he do this to me? The doctor said not yet. I can barely breathe. There are so many of them. I shudder. I watch in slow motion horror as he eases the door of the first room open. I can feel the mist fogging my brain and then a sharp tap on my cheek makes me open my eyes.

All I see at first are bare buttocks and thighs, strapped tightly to some kind of apparatus. From the back of the knees to the neck are red welts. I hear a faint, satisfied. "Ah," behind me as we move forward. I can't take my eyes from the form in front of me. It's ghastly. It's horrible. We proceed further into the room. I see two terrified eyes above a vicious gag. It's Mrs. Porto. I sag and strong arms support me.

I hear Mister Caldwell's voice apologizing for me. "She has been damaged by this one. Thankfully not completely. She isn't wholly healed yet and still weak." His words are so casual as if he were discussing an article in the paper. I see the woman wince in pain as hands of the men prod and explore. I try to swallow. I can't. I seem to be in shock. I see what is going on in front of me but can't react.

She is bent over a wooden trestle and stretched out tight, her arms manacled and attached to the wall in front of her. Her legs and belly are tightly strapped to it. Her breasts are red and swollen and hang down freely. Her legs are spread wide. I see the men laughing as they prod her with their fingers in her ass and vagina. I can barely stand. A hand grabs and squeezes her breast cruelly and I hear the muted scream. I see small drops of blood trickle from her mouth. This can't be real. He said this is who hurt me. I can't take it in.

The Sheik walks around her, the other men draw back. He prods and pokes. I see her writhe against the pain as he touches and pushes on her welts. He shoves what appears to be his whole fist up her cunt and again I hear the muted groans of pain. He yanks her cheeks apart and I see his brows raise in surprise.

"It is probably virgin," Mister Caldwell says with a sinister smile. He reaches out and strokes her hair absently. "You see Mrs. Porto doesn't like men. The name is just a sort of camouflage. She prefers women. As you can see I gave her another reason not to like us this afternoon," he says, running his fingers over the welts. "I don't think she has ever felt a man in her backside. Of course she has used dildos with her lovers but as you can see by the tightness, her ass still looks virgin."

"Not for long. Eastern men prefer this method than the other. It is always tighter, especially after they are allowed to give birth. It is a good way to remind them of their submission to us. As for her liking women that is easily controlled. A few quick snips in the right place and she will not wish for any, male or female, but will be used as I please. Her only thought from this moment on will be to please her master so to save her skin."

I sway when I see the desperate clenching as she tries to tighten against the possibility. I remember the pain she caused me but still felt nothing but a helpless pity for her. The Arab's smile widens. It sends chills down my spine. "We must not deprive her of any experience my friend. I am to understand this is a permanent gift?"

"Of course," Mister Caldwell accedes. I watch the man pull up his robes and place the hard knob against her tight opening. No lubrication, I think to myself and then I see him ram it in with one powerful thrust. I see her muscles strain, I hear her scream of agony behind the gag and I'm reliving my own nightmare. I turn and grab Mister Caldwell's lapels and bury my head into his chest. I'm shaking so hard, my teeth chatter. Her mewings of pain echo through my brain, over and over and I'm not sure if it's me and it's happening again or if it's her. I hear my name and then nothing.

I wake up over his lap on the couch. I can tell immediately by the tension in his thighs under me that he is furious. I have embarrassed him in front of guests. I raise my head and see white robes all around and then his hand is pounding my backside. The pain catches me unaware, the humiliation is worse. I hear the chuckles, the murmurs of satisfaction. I try not to cry out but I do eventually and only then does he stop. He makes me lay there, exposed to all as they converse and partake of the hors d'oeuvres.

I hear the deep voice of the Sheik. "You are a tolerant master Mister Caldwell."

"Only because of her poor health lately."

"Has she give you children yet?"

"No. But that is because it is how I wish it. Maybe in a few years. She is young and has much to learn."

He allows me to rise only when dinner is served. I cannot meet anyone's eyes. I feel the blush cover my cheeks and hear the amused laughter. I must sit through the interminable meal and eat. I am all too aware of my backside that is on fire.

I'm not expected to converse or entertain and I am thankful for it. All during the meal one of the men rises and departs when another returns. Once or twice I hear the unmistakable sound of the lash hitting flesh and it is all I can do to keep my food down.

Words flow around me, some in English, some in Arabic. I don't listen. I concentrate on trying to chew and swallow. My throat is tight. I don't know how I continue but I do as if I were an automaton.

"It is a shame about M. Lafouche and his son is it not?" The words penetrate and my hand freezes halfway to my mouth. I suddenly can't breathe.

"Not an uncommon thing. I don't like those small private planes. I much prefer the larger jets."

"I agree my friend. I understand there was someone else with them. One of his employee's no doubt."

I raise my eyes slowly and see Mister Caldwell's boring into mine steadily. I know what he will say before he utters the words. "I understand it was someone from an employment agency."

My fork clatters onto my plate and I hastily mumble an apology. Silence reigns for a brief moment and then the conversation resumes around me. Everyone who knew of my circumstances is gone. The former president and his vice-president died in a mysterious car accident. The employment agency man and the Lafouche's in a plane accident. Mrs. Porto will leave tomorrow for far away lands and never be in a position to talk to anyone. Mister Su knew nothing definite and had been painfully warned. The Sheik and his men don't consider these circumstances anything unusual. In fact they heartily approve of them.

I am numb. Completely. This is a turning point. The relationship has changed again but this time I understand it. The message is clear. I belong to him. Totally. All the loose ends have been taken care of. There is no one left who knows about me. No one to think about me and wonder. All my choices are gone. Did I ever have any?

I feel panic building and then it is replaced by a strange peacefulness. No more wondering. No more questions. I've been given an answer. My life is in his hands. It is a strange type of freedom. A frightening type of freedom yet somehow deep down I think I always knew it.

I raise my eyes and see him watching me steadily. He knows I know. His lazy smile tells me he knows I've accepted it. I find myself smiling back.

The Sheik interrupts our mental communion. "I have missed something my friend?"

Mister Caldwell smiles and takes his eyes from mine. "My little love bird has just accepted that she will have her wings clipped."

"They all do eventually."

"Yes, especially when they have no choice," He rises and bows slightly to the men at the table. "If you will excuse us." His hand raises and I take it. He leads me down a hall. I hear the rise and fall of the lash, I hear the grunts of a man's satisfaction as we pass a door. We stop in front of his bedroom door.

He opens it and the first thing I see is the cabinet. His room is dark with massive heavy furniture. A true Victorian gentleman's room. My dress is removed along with my stockings. "Come to me Miss Julia."

I do. I kneel when he touches my shoulder. I release his penis and suck it into my mouth. I feel him bend slightly forward. "It is time to resume your training." The words end and then I feel the sting of the crop across my backside. I just try harder to please him.

Available now

The Captive
by Anonymous

When a wealthy Enlish man-about-town attempts to make advances to the beautiful twenty-year-old debutante Caroline Martin, she haughtily repels him. As revenge, he pays a white-slavery ring £30,000 to have Caroline abducted and spirited away to the remote Atlas Mountains of Morocco. There the mistress of the ring and her sinister assistant Jason begin Caroline's education—an abduction designed to break her will and prepare her for her mentor.

Available now

Captive II
by Richard Manton

Following the best-selling novel, *The Captive*, this sequel is set among the subtropical provinces of Cheluna, where white slavery remains an institution to this day. Brigid, with her dancing girl figure and sweeping tresses of red hair, has caused the prosecution of a rich admirer. As retribution, he employs the underground organization Rio 9 to abduct and transport her to Cambina Alta Plantation. Naked and bound before the Sadism of Col. Manrique and the perversities of the Comte de Zantra, Brigid endures an education in submission. Her training continues until she is ready to be the slave of the man who has chosen her.

Available now

Captive III: The Perfumed Trap
by Anonymous

The story of slavery and passionate training described first-hand in the spirited correspondence of two wealthy cousins, Alec and Miriam. The power wielded by them over the girls who cross their paths leads them beyond Cheluna to the remote settlement of Cambina Alta and a life of plantation discipline. On the way, Alec's passion for Julie, a golden-haired nymph, is rivaled by Miriam's disciplinary zeal for Jenny, a rebellious young woman under correction at a police barracks.

Available now

Captive IV: The Eyes Behind the Mask
by Anonymous

The Captives of Cheluna feel a dread fascination for the boy whose duty it is to chastise. This narrative follows a masked apprentice who obeys his master's orders without pity or restraint. Emma Smith's birching would cause a reform school scandal. Secret additions to the frenzy of nineteen-year-old Karen and Noreen mingle the boy's fierce passion with lascivious punishment. Mature young women like Jenny Woodward pay dearly for defying their master, whose masked servant also prints the marks of slavery on Lesley Hollingsworth, following *Captive II*. The untrained and the self-assured alike learn to shiver, as they lie waiting, under the caress of the eyes behind the mask.

Available now

Captive V: The Soundproof Dream
by Richard Manton

Beauty lies in bondage everywhere in the tropical island of Cheluna. Joanne, a 19-year old rebel, is sent to detention on Krater Island where obedience and discipline occupy the secret hours of night. Like the dark beauty Shirley Wood and blond shopgirl Maggie Turnbull, Jo is subjected to unending punishment. When her Krater Island training is complete, Jo's fate is Metron, the palace home of the strange Colonel Mantrique.

ALSO IN THE IRONWOOD SERIES

Available now

Images of Ironwood
by Don Winslow

Ironwood. The very name of that unique institution remains strongly evocative, even to this day. In this, the third volume of the famous Ironwood trilogy, the reader is once again invited to share in the Ironwood experience. *Images of Ironwood* presents selected scenes of unrelenting sensuality, of erotic longing, and occasionally, of those bizarre proclivities which touch the outer fringe of human sexuality.

In these pages we renew our acquaintance with James, the lusty entrepreneur who now directs the Ironwood enterprise; with his bevy of young female students being trained in the many ways of love; and with Cora Blasingdale, the cold remote mistress of discipline. The images presented here capture the essence of the Ironwood experience.

Available Now

Ironwood
by Don Winslow

The harsh reality of disinheritance and poverty vanish from the world of our young narrator, James, when he discovers he's in line for a choice position at an exclusive and very strict school for girls. Ironwood becomes for him a fantastic dream world where discipline knows few boundaries, and where his role as master affords him free reign with the willing, well-trained and submissive young beauties in his charge. As overseer of Ironwood, Cora Blasingdale is well-equipped to keep her charges in line. Under her guidance the saucy girls are put through their paces and tamed. And for James, it seems, life has just begun.

TITLES IN THE SHADOW LANE SERIES FROM BLUE MOON BOOKS

Available now

SHADOW LANE

In a small New England village, four spirited young women explore the romance of discipline with their lovers. Laura's husband is handsome but terribly strict, leaving her no choice but to rebel. Damaris is a very bad girl until detective Flagg takes her in hand. Susan simultaneously begins her freshman year at college and her odyssey in the scene with two charming older men. Marguerite can't decide whether to remain dreamily submissive or become a goddess.

Available now

SHADOW LANE II
Return to Random Point

All Susan Ross ever wanted was a handsome and masterful lover who would turn her over his knee now and then without trying to control her life. She ends up with three of them in this second installment of the ongoing chronicle of romantic discipline, set in a village on Cape Cod.

Available now

SHADOW LANE III
The Romance of Discipline

Mischievous Susan Ross, now at Vassar, continues to exasperate Anthony Newton, while pursuing other dominant men. Heroically proportioned Michael Flagg proves capable but bossy, while handsome Marcus Gower has one too many demands. Dominating her girlfriend Diana brings Susan unexpected satisfaction, but playing top is work and so she turns her submissive over to the boys. Susan then inspires her adoring servant Dennis to revolt against his own submissive nature and turn his young mistress over his knee.

Available now

SHADOW LANE IV
The Chronicles of Random Point

Ever since the fifties, spanking has been practiced for the pleasure of adults in Random Point. The present era finds Hugo Sands at the center of its scene. Formerly a stern and imperious dom, his persistent love for Laura has all but civilized him. But instead of enchanting his favorite submissive, Hugo's sudden tameness has the opposite effect on Laura, who breaks every rule of their relationship to get him to behave like the strict martinet she once knew and loved. Meanwhile ivy league brat Susan Ross selects Sherman Cooper as the proper dominant to give her naughty friend Diana Stratton to and all the girls of Random Point conspire to rescue a delightful submissive from a cruel master.

Available now

SHADOW LANE V
The Spanking Persuasion

When Patricia's addiction to luxury necessitates a rescue from Hugo Sands, repayment is exacted in the form of discipline from one of the world's most implacable masters. Carter compels Aurora to give up her professional B&D lifestyle, not wholly through the use of a hairbrush. Marguerite takes a no-nonsense young husband, with predictable results. Sloan finds the girl of his dreams is more like the brat of his nightmares. Portia pushes Monty quite beyond control in trying to prove he's a switch. The stories are interconnected and share a theme: bad girls get spanked!

Sadistic Impulse
by Jack Spender

Professor Jack Spender is hired to teach a group of amoral sorority honeys in the French Riviera, but must also regiment their heedless sexual frolics under the brooding, lustful shadow of the Marquis de Sade. More devastating yet, Spender knows that beneath the surface glitz and fleshly opulence of the Azure Coast lies older traditions of Greek orgiastic rites. Continuing his passion for the beautiful Mlle. Kore, he finds a "yearning libidinal welcome rooted in the very earth itself."

Eveline II
by Anonymous

Eveline II continues the delightfully erotic tale of a defiant aristocratic young English woman who throws off the mantle of respectability in order to revel in life's sexual pleasures. After returning to her paternal home in London in order to escape the boredom of marriage, she plunges with total abandon into self-indulgence and begins to "convert" other young ladies to her wanton ways.

Elaine Cox
by Richard Manton

Elaine Cox is an adolescent tomboy of short skirts, bare thighs and snub-nosed insolence. Her misconduct puts her under the command of her middle-aged admirer, and as punishment and seduction alternate, a dark romance begins in the soundless vaults and tiled discipline rooms. Soon Elaine is a tomboy well-chastised, the recipient of passionate punishments.

Slaves of the Hypnotist
by Anonymous

Harry, son of a well-to-do English country family, has set out to "conquer" all the females within his immediate reach. But no sooner does he begin his exploits than he encounters the imperious beauty, Davina, who enslaves him through her remarkable power of hypnotism. Thus entranced, Harry indulges in every aspect of eroticism known to man or woman.

ORDER FORM

Attach a separate sheet for additional titles.

Title	Quantity	Price
____________	____	____
____________	____	____
____________	____	____
____________	____	____

Shipping and Handling (see charges below) ________

Sales tax (in CA and NY) ________

Total ________

Name ____________________

Address ____________________

City ____________ State ________ Zip ________

Daytime telephone number ____________________

❑ Check ❑ Money Order (US dollars only. No COD orders accepted.)

Credit Card # ____________________ Exp. Date ________

❑ MC ❑ VISA ❑ AMEX

Signature ____________________

(if paying with a credit card you must sign this form.)

Shipping and Handling charges:*

Domestic: $4 for 1st book, $.75 each additional book. International: $5 for 1st book, $1 each additional book
*rates in effect at time of publication. Subject to Change.

Mail order to Publishers Group West, Attention: Order Dept., 1700 Fourth St., Berkeley, CA 94710, or fax to (510) 528-3444.

PLEASE ALLOW 4-6 WEEKS FOR DELIVERY. ALL ORDERS SHIP VIA 4TH CLASS MAIL.

Look for Blue Moon Books at your favorite local bookseller or from your favorite online bookseller.